MAN WHO COULD WORK MIRACLES

THE MACMILLAN COMPANY
NEW YORK · BOSTON · CHICAGO · DALLAS
ATLANTA · SAN FRANCISCO

MAN WHO COULD WORK MIRACLES

A Film by H. G. WELLS

Based on the short story entitled

THE MAN WHO COULD WORK

MIRACLES

1936 — THE MACMILLAN COMPANY — NEW YORK

PRINTED IN THE UNITED STATES OF AMERICA
BY THE STRATFORD PRESS, INC., NEW YORK

CONTENTS

Introductory Remarks

THIS is a film of imaginative comedy. It is framed in a Brief Prologue and Epilogue, which point to its larger intimations. George McWhirter Fotheringay is a definite personality, a concrete human being, and from beginning to end he remains *himself*. All the characters are highly individualised characters—not symbols. They have to be *acted*. We put the Frame about this story to guard ourselves against the invasion (which will be fatal) during production of any weakening "symbolism" in sets, make up, music, dialogue or any other detail of production. All that must be real, real as can be, "actual," matter-of-fact, up to the last phase of the world catastrophe. The Frame on the other hand has to be as "sublime" as music and camera can make it. The Frame could be stripped off and the film would still remain a coherent imaginative story, but the Frame is necessary to broaden out the reference and make *Man who could work Miracles* a proper companion piece to *Things to Come*.

Note that the "end" rests on Fotheringay and not on the Frame. Fotheringay is *it*. In contrast with *Things to Come* this is a star film.

INTRODUCTORY REMARKS

The Music

THERE should be a steady flow of sustaining music to this film, gay passing into the grotesque and rising to immense passages of stormy sound. There should be characteristic motifs to sustain certain special threads of interest.

Fotheringay for instance ought to have a cheerful, trivial, tripping, catching air (with a lurking possibility of pathos). He could sometimes whistle this air between his teeth in moments of indecision. Linked with this there should be a distinct flourish for his miracles—petty and comic at first and later, as the miracles increase in importance, becoming charged with portent and menace.

Even when there are long rhetorical speeches the music should be keeping on with its quiet comment as if a goblin orchestra was watching and enjoying the drama, ready to stand up in excitement at the stormy parts.

The introduction should have a certain calm grandeur which becomes troubled by a sort of throbbing and ends abruptly in a loud silence when the finger descends upon Fotheringay.

Throbbing in the music has not yet been adequately exploited in the cinema to enhance an approaching climax. It ought to be tried here.

THE FILM

MAN WHO COULD WORK MIRACLES

PART I

The Elemental Powers

GRANDIOSE music.

The starry sky is seen as it might be seen on a clear frosty night in the temperate zone. At first *the arrangement of stars is unfamiliar.* There are strange nebulæ and two very bright constellations of seven and eleven stars respectively. At first the stars stream slowly across the screen while the Riders ride. Then at the point indicated by the letter A the familiar constellations appear, but somewhat flattened, distorted and foreshortened. At the point indicated by letter B they fall into place exactly as they are known to us—Orion high in the heavens.

Across the stars two Riders become more and more distinct. They are beautiful, naked, male figures on horses. They are at first thinly luminous and then they become opaque. The stars shine brightly through them, then the two Riders become more opaque and definite, so as to blot out the stars behind them. They give the effect of being bronze rather than flesh and blood. Their voices are heard, but it is not quite clear which speaks. The First Rider is called here the Observer. The Second Rider is called the Indifference. A third great ele-

3

mental is named the Player or the Giver of Power. These names do not appear on the screen. They are unimportant, and are used here for convenience only.

The OBSERVER: "Our brother the Giver of Power is yonder, playing with his planet." Points.

The INDIFFERENCE: "That queer small planet with the live things upon it?"

He looks under his hand to shade his eyes from a bright star cluster close above them.

The OBSERVER: "Let us see what he is doing."

Here is the point A.

The great shapes of the two Riders pass forward across the screen, their horses sink down out of sight so that the observer and the indifference become the semi-transparent half-length bodies of mounted men to the left and right of the central figure. They come to rest in semi-profile to the audience, looking at the central figure. This is a third great shadowy shape, also of heroic form and beauty. He sits in an attitude recalling Rodin's Thinker, brooding over something between his feet. (This is the point B.) Between his feet, at first infinitely small, is the solar system. It becomes larger and, as it does, the two other Riders pass by extension out of the screen and so become mere voices. But the player is still there, shadowy, but now almost opaque, and filling the screen so that only the solar system and a few near stars can be seen between and through his feet.

The INDIFFERENCE: "Cannot you leave those nasty little animals alone?"

The PLAYER shakes his head. "These men?"

4

The OBSERVER: "They are such silly little creatures. Swarming and crawling. Why has the Master permitted them?"

The PLAYER: "They are pitifully small and weak. But —I like them."

The INDIFFERENCE: "What is the good of them? Squash them."

The PLAYER, after a pause: "No, I like them."

The OBSERVER: "Nonsense. They are nasty. They are mean and cruel and stupid. They are vain and greedy. They crawl over each other and kill and devour each other."

The PLAYER: "They are just weak."

The INDIFFERENCE: "Happily."

The PLAYER: "If they were not weak they might not be so pitiful. But their lives are so short and their efforts so feeble. . . ."

The OBSERVER: "If they had Power they would be no better."

The PLAYER: "I am going to try that—I am going to give them all the Power I can."

The OBSERVER: "Don't. You are the Power-giver. You can give Power beyond measure. What will happen if these greedy, silly, human scabs, who can only breed and scramble, spread out among our stars?"

The PLAYER: "You will see."

The OBSERVER: "Are you going to give all of them Power?"

The Player nods and smiles with his head looking down on the earth.

The OBSERVER: "But *limitless* Power? Power to do *anything?*"

The PLAYER: "There is a limit to the Power I can give. So the Master has decreed. . . . There is a bit of gritty stuff at the heart of every individual, no Power can touch. The Soul—the Individuality—that ultimate mystery only the Master can control. Their Wills—such as they are—are Free. But all else—every position, every circumstance is mine. . . ."

The solar system slowly expands so that the Player also passes beyond the scope of the screen and becomes merely a voice. The three voices come from above and right and left. The solar system now occupies the main part of the screen against a background of stars.

The OBSERVER: "Now we shall see what their Souls amount to!"

The PLAYER: "The Will of Man—released!"

The OBSERVER: "Worms rampant."

The INDIFFERENCE: "They will defile the stars."

The OBSERVER: "Don't give Power to all of them. That would be an explosion. Try one or two first. Try just one."

The PLAYER: "That might not work."

The OBSERVER: "Try just one—and see what there is in the human heart."

The INDIFFERENCE: "Yes. Try one. Someone commonplace. A fair sample. Let him be able to do—anything. Give him the Power to work miracles—without limit."

The PLAYER musingly: "Why not? Then perhaps we might see."

The solar system has been coming nearer and grow-

6

ing larger. By this time the earth is recognisable, coming into the foreground of the picture. The three heads appear close together, looking gravely down on the planet.

The PLAYER: "Just any little fellow. They are all very much alike. I'll take one haphazard."

He puts out his finger slowly towards the earth.

The earth grows larger against the starry heavens. The hand with its projecting finger, overwhelmingly large, approaches the little earth.

PART II

The Gift

MUSIC ("the music of the spheres") has been going on very faintly as the voices speak. It becomes more audible as the latter sentences are spoken and now rises to, or rather degenerates into an anxious, disturbing, protesting air and ends abruptly—to suggest such a dismayed apprehensive silence as might precede the putting of a spark to a magazine.

Then a church clock strikes nine.

Under a starry sky, Dewhinton, a little English country town, is seen, dimly lit with a few gas lamps, lit-windows, road signs, etc. The camera trucks up to, into and through this and comes to a stop outside a public house. The street is deserted except for Mr. George Mc-Whirter Fotheringay, who approaches the inn in a leisurely manner. He is a commonplace, pale-faced young man, assistant in the general store. In the stillness a beam of blackness in the shape of a finger tip descends upon the bowler hat of Mr. Fotheringay. It is held for a moment, a beam of blackness with a pulsating flicker in its darkness, as though obscure currents of Power were flowing down it. Then it fades out. Mr. Fotherin-

8

gay is not apparently affected by this, or aware of it in any way. He pauses before the door, adjusts his hat and stick, and enters. As he opens the door there is a warm swell of argumentative voices.

PART III

The First Miracle

THE Long Dragon Inn, Dewhinton. It is the sort of inn to be found near the centre of any English small town. The scene is the Bar Parlour. The chief light is a large paraffin lamp hanging by a hook from the ceiling.

Mr. Fotheringay has established himself in a leaning attitude against the bar. Facing him is a sturdy individual, Mr. Toddy Beamish, a builder in a small way. Behind the bar, wiping out a glass, is the rather portly barmaid, Miss Maybridge. Mr. Cox, the landlord, is in shirt-sleeves and rather in the background. A cyclist sits at a table to the left nearly under the lamp, listening with an air of profound inattention to the discussion. An old man with a dog by a table to the right, is wagging his head slowly from side to side with a certain air of disapproval. Shots fairly close up to the speakers.

TODDY BEAMISH: "Well, Mr. Fotheringay, *you* may not believe in Miracles—but I do. Not to believe in Miracles, I say, strikes at the very roots of religion."

Old man assents.

MISS MAYBRIDGE: "Of course, Mr. Beamish, there's Miracles—*and* Miracles."

FOTHERINGAY: "Exactly, Miss Maybridge. Now let's

10

get clear what a miracle is. Some people would argue the sun rising every day is a miracle."

TODDY BEAMISH: "Some of us do."

FOTHERINGAY: "Not what I call a miracle. A miracle I say is something *contrariwise* to the usual course of nature done by power of will—something what couldn't happen—not without being specially willed."

TODDY BEAMISH: "So *you* say."

FOTHERINGAY: "Well, you got to 'ave a definition." (Appeals to cyclist.) "What do *you* say, sir?"

Cyclist starts, clears his throat and expresses assent.

Fotheringay appeals to landlord Cox.

COX: "I'm not *in* this."

TODDY BEAMISH: "Well, I agree. Contrariwise to the usual course of nature. 'Ave it so. And what about it?"

FOTHERINGAY, pursuing his argument: "For instance. Here would be a miracle. The lamp here in the natural course of nature couldn't burn like that upsy-down, could it, Mr. Beamish?"

TODDY BEAMISH: *"You* say it couldn't."

FOTHERINGAY: "And you? Wah!—you don't mean to say—No?"

TODDY BEAMISH: "No. Well, it couldn't."

FOTHERINGAY: "Very well. Then here comes someone, as it might be me, along here, and he stands as it might be here, and he says to this lamp, as I might do, collecting all my will—and I'm doing it, mind you—I'm playing fair: 'Turn upsy-down, I tell you, without breaking, and go on burning steady and—' Ooer!"

The lamp obeys.

Close up of Mr. Fotheringay's amazement. He keeps his hand held out. Mouth open.

Scene of general consternation. The cyclist, who is nearly under the lamp, realises danger, ducks and darts away. Miss Maybridge, polishing a glass in happy unconsciousness, turns, sees the amazing thing and screams. MR. COX, open-mouthed, says: " 'Ere! What the 'ell?" The old man's dog gets up and barks. The old man's apprehension of the situation comes slowly.

Close up of Mr. Fotheringay in a profuse perspiration. "It's not possible," he gasps. "I can't keep it up—it's *got* to drop."

The lamp falls and smashes chimney and shade. But there is no fire. The container of the lamp is a metal one and the paraffin is not spilt. The bar is in darkness until Cox brings another lamp from an inner room.

COX, with dangerous calm: "And now, Mr. Fotheringay, will you be so good as to explain this silly trick—before I chuck you out."

The CYCLIST, much agitated: "Silliest thing I've ever seen done."

TODDY BEAMISH: "Whatever made you do it?"

COX: "Outside is the place for you. Outside the Long Dragon for good and all."

MISS MAYBRIDGE: " 'E's got to pay for two bitters, Mr. Cox."

COX: "And he's going to pay for a lamp-shade and chimney."

The OLD MAN suddenly breaking into a shout: " 'E did it with wires. I knowed a girl once who did things like that. A bad girl she was—my *Lord!* Wires he did it with."

MR. FOTHERINGAY, recovering the power of speech: "Look here, Mr. Cox, I don't know what happened to that confounded lamp—more than anyone. I didn't touch it. I *swear* I didn't touch it."

Close up of incredulous faces as Fotheringay sees them.

MR. COX, particularly implacable: "Look you here, Mr. Conjurer, don't let's have any more pother. You get out of my house before I shift you. . . ."

PART IV

Period of Realisation

THE vista of the village street lit not very brightly by gas lamps. MR. FOTHERINGAY, with his collar torn and his tie disarranged, is going home. He stops under a lamp. Close up of his face. "But what was it *'appened?* I don't understand what 'appened."

He continues on his way. Stops under another lamp. "Yes—but what *did* 'appen?" A man puzzled profoundly. His face under a third lamp. He makes movements of the hands to recall the movement of the lamp.

Scene shifts to Mr. Fotheringay's bedroom in his lodging. A small, cheap, lodging-house room lit by a candle. Mr. Fotheringay has taken off coat and waistcoat and is removing his collar and tie. "No need for Mr. Cox to get violent."

He inspects the state of the buttonhole of his collar and puts collar and tie very carefully over the small square shabby looking-glass. He sinks into profound thought.

"*I* didn't want the confounded lamp to upset."

14

He begins to have inklings of how things are. His lips repeat arguments noiselessly.

"Miracles. . . . It was just when I said, ' 'Ere, you be turned upsy-down!' "

He starts with a sudden thought. He stares a prolonged stare at the candle beside him. He makes as if to speak and does not do so. He lifts a hand, half-pointing to the candle, and drops it irresolutely. He is evidently afraid of the possible success of the experiment he contemplates. At last he says: " 'Ere. You be lifted up about a foot."

The burning candle is lifted up.

FOTHERINGAY: "Now—now—now—don't lose your head, George McWhirter Fotheringay, don't lose your head. It isn't going to drop if you don't let it down." Watches it almost appealingly. "No. . . ."

FOTHERINGAY: "Now, keep burning steady, don't drop any nasty grease about or we shall get into trouble, and now over you go, upsy-down."

The burning candle obeys.

FOTHERINGAY's confirmatory grimace: he is beginning to realise his mastery. Almost casually he says: "As you were—on the table."

Candle behaves as directed.

FOTHERINGAY sits down amazed: "Gaw! It's a miracle! It's really a blooming miracle. Why? one might make any amount of money on the music 'alls with a trick like this."

He meditates: "I suppose I could do it to almost anything. The table? 'Ere!"

He gesticulates and speaks inaudibly. The table is raised up.

FOTHERINGAY considers the things on it: "Too risky to turn it over. Go down again." It does so with a bump. "Now—the bed?"

He regards the bed doubtfully. "Biggish." Then with a gesture of "Here goes" he addresses himself to the bed. It is raised.

FOTHERINGAY: "Don't bump on the floor, mind. Down you go—*quietly*."

FOTHERINGAY meditates: "Raising things—by will power."

He goes to the looking-glass, sticks out his chin and glares. "Will power. 'Ipnotism and all that. Now I wonder. . . ."

He raises himself a foot or so—is obviously rather frightened and comes down again.

"Wonder what else I might be able to do."

He fiddles with the extinguisher of the candlestick. "'Ere, get big. Be one of those cones what conjurers have. See."

If possible, the extinguisher must *grow* to a cone. If not, it must change to one in Fotheringay's hand.

FOTHERINGAY: "Now, let's get something." He puts it down on the table and turns up his sleeves conjurer fashion. "Hey presto!"

Nothing happens. He speaks louder: "Hey presto! Let there be a kitten under this." He lifts the cone with a gesture. He addresses an imaginary audience: "You see, Ladies and Gentlemen! A healthy young kitten!"

The kitten looks round and jumps off the table.

FOTHERINGAY: " 'Ere, Pussy. Pussy!"

He pursues the kitten which darts under the bed. Fotheringay scratches his cheek in consternation. "Can't let her go there. These kittens! If it makes a mess there'll be the devil to pay with Ma Wilkins! 'Ere, Pussy! Diddums." He bends down calling: "Pussy! Pussy!" and presently scrambles under the bed. His feet are seen kicking about. "Come 'ere, I say." Kitten is heard spitting. "Drat it! You little *beast*."

He emerges ruefully and kneels up, examining his bleeding hand which is scratched. "Rotten little pincushion!" Is struck by an idea. Goes on all fours. Points. " 'Ere, you. Be changed into a pincushion. Ah—*got* you!" He draws out a cat-shaped pincushion from under the bed. He regards it curiously and then puts it back under the cone. "Presto vanish!"

FOTHERINGAY to the cone: "Now, you be an extinguisher again and we won't say any more about *that*. No."

FOTHERINGAY meditates, sucking his scratches. "Got to be careful."

A fresh idea. " 'Ere, you scratches—be cured."

FOTHERINGAY: "Lor! I could go on doing miracles all night, I suppose."

Clock strikes eleven.

FOTHERINGAY: "Bed-time, George McWhirter—bedtime."

He sits down on his bed and begins to unlace a shoe.

FOTHERINGAY: "Most 'stonishing thing that ever happened to me."

A later shot of the bedroom with Mr. Fotheringay in bed. The candle has burnt down to the candlestick. The bed is littered with two or three small rabbits, bunches of flowers, a walking-stick, a number of watches, two china cats. He is eating a bunch of (miraculous) grapes rather suspiciously.

The village clock strikes two.

"Crimes! it's two o'clock in the morning and I shall be late for shop. What shall I do with all this litter? 'Ere, all I've got 'ere by magic, *vanish*." (They vanish.) "Gollys! I've burnt my candle to a stump. Old Mother Wilkins won't half talk in the morning."

He blows at the guttering, flaring candle. It will not go out until at last he says: "Oh, *go* out."

Instant darkness except for the dim window. The bed creaks.

PART V

Mr. Fotheringay Perplexed

ALARM clock ringing. Church clock strikes seven. Burlesque Dawn music.

Fotheringay waking up. Stretches. Rubs his eyes. Starts up into a sitting position.

"It was a dream."

Questions himself mutely. Scratches cheek.

Makes the characteristic gesture for a miracle. Lips move.

A small rabbit appears on the counterpane and is vanished again.

"Gollys! It's *true.*"

Makes a resolution. "I won't do any more of it—not for a day. No. I'll think it over. . . . Won't do. Miracles coming off your fingers before you hardly know. *No,* Mr. George McWhirter Fotheringay, it's going to make no end of trouble for you—if you don't watch it."

Fotheringay at breakfast.

His breakfast egg is bad. Smells it and looks resentful. He changes it into another. Has two more. Perplexity. "She'll want to know how the shells came 'ere. Where can I put them? Lord, it's going to be difficult. *I* know!

19

'Ere, you two shells, be changed into house flies and be off with you. . . . Not a bad way that."

Church clock strikes eight. Mr. Fotheringay rouses himself to depart—still very thoughtful.

Exterior of the premises of Grigsby and Blott, General Drapers. Bill Stoker is seen in the large window dressing it. He is a conspicuously good-looking young man rather on the florid side, much handsomer than Fotheringay. Ada Price, the costume young lady, stands in the doorway between the window space and the shop floor and is conversing (inaudibly) with him. She is tall and dark and wears the long figure-displaying dress of the Costume Room. Her manner is coquettish. Stoker bends down as if to say something intimate to her. Fotheringay appears in street outside. A start of jealousy. They become aware of him. Ada Price hastily assumes an expression of blameless dignity. Informal greetings. Fotheringay enters shop.

The Haberdashery Department. Miss Maggie Hooper, a blonde of rich sentimental possibilities, with large dreamy blue eyes, is wearing her arm in a sling. Her very much freckled junior, EFFIE BRICKMAN, asks: "How's the arm, Miss Hooper?"

"Not so painful so long as I keep it in the sling and don't use it. I wear the sling to remind me. Oh, I'm so hungry to-day—I wish it was lunch."

EFFIE: "I haven't the heart for lunch."

MISS HOOPER: "Feeling ill?"

EFFIE: "Feeling freckled—freckled all over. I've got two more. Powder's no use, Maggie. I'd be *all* powder. And *he's* nasty about it. Oh well, never mind—what can't be cured must be endured. Who's *this* sneaking round from the Manchester?"

MISS HOOPER: "Good mind to give him the cold shoulder."

EFFIE: "Only you can't. *I* know."

MISS HOOPER: "Oh, I could. But I don't want to."

EFFIE: "Two's company and three's none. I'm off."

MISS HOOPER: "You needn't go."

EFFIE: "Only I will. See?"

As she disappears Mr. Fotheringay comes along behind the counter. It is against the rules for him to desert his department, but this is the slack time of the day before the afternoon customers come in.

MISS HOOPER: "You don't often come to the Haberdashery nowadays, Mr. Fotheringay. New attraction in the Costumes, I presume. Oh, we know all about it."

FOTHERINGAY, fatuous smirk: "I keep my heart in this department, Miss Hooper."

"Reely?"

"Reely. D'you know I've been wanting to talk to you all day. All the morning."

"Reely?"

"Serious. Maggie. . . . Something—something queer's happened to me. I can't make head or tail of it."

MISS HOOPER: "Not been left money or won a lottery ticket?"

Fotheringay shakes his head.

"Something queer? Not fallen in love?"

"That happened long ago—as well you know, Miss Hooper."

"Reely?"

"Reely."

Archness on both sides.

"They say you had more than was good for you at the Long Dragon last night and upset a lamp. It can't be *that?*"

"Well, it *is* about that. In a way. You see it's odd. It's like this. If I say let a thing happen, *it happens.*"

"Sort of prophesy?"

"No—sort of miracle."

"Oh, go—*on.*"

"No, truth, Maggie; I'll prove it. Look 'ere."

Creates a bunch of violets and hands it to her.

"Of course, that's a trick, Mr. Fotheringay. One of your sleight of hand tricks. But they're lovely violets. They reely are. You didn't get this bunch for sixpence, I know. It's a good trick. They just seemed to jump out of nothing. But if only one *could* work miracles. Just think of what you could do."

"F'rinstance?"

"Heal the sick."

"I never thought of that. Leastways—I *did* heal some scratches."

"Here's my sprained arm. What wouldn't I give just to lift things and put them away—and not think of it."

FOTHERINGAY: *"Well."*

He touches her arm: "Be all right. Lift it."

The arm is tried. Incredulity at first. "Mr. Fotheringay, you're a healer! You've got the gift of healing."

FOTHERINGAY: "It ain't everything I've got."

"But the *good* you might do!"

"I s'pose I might. P'raps I will."

22

Miss Hooper twists her arm about. There is no doubt about the miracle.

"Now, there's Effie there—heartbroken about her freckles. Her fellow hates freckles and she keeps on getting fresh ones. Well,—"

"I'll try."

MISS HOOPER: calls Effie, who appears. "D'you know Mr. Fotheringay has a charm for freckles? He has. Do, do it, Mr. Fotheringay."

FOTHERINGAY: "Let all the freckles go" (hastily adds) "and your complexion be perfect."

Change.

MISS HOOPER: *"Oh!* Where's a mirror?"

Mirror.

EFFIE: "It's marvellous. How he did it, I *don't* know."

FOTHERINGAY: "And *I* don't know."

Bell rings. "There's the second course for dinner."

Scene: the dining room of Messrs. Grigsby and Blott. The midday dinner in progress. Passing of plates down a long table, etc. Fotheringay is in a central position, next to him is Miss Maggie Hooper and next beyond Miss Ada Price. Bill Stoker sits with his back to audience. And sideways is Effie of the dazzling complexion. A junior apprentice and others. At the head of the table sits the Housekeeper.

FOTHERINGAY talks: "How it came to me, I don't know. I just say to a thing: you be so and so or you do so and so, and it seems to happen. Maybe it's will power. I never dreamt I had it in me until last night."

BILL STOKER: "When you broke the lamp in the Long Dragon. We've heard of that."

HOUSEKEEPER: "Well, don't you go breaking anything here, Mr. Fotheringay. No miracles in the house *or* the shop. Please. This is a drapery establishment—not a Home of Magic."

MISS HOOPER: "But he cured my sprain! And look at *her.*"

Admiration of Effie, who turns her head graciously.

HOUSEKEEPER: "All the same, it isn't wise. Major Grigsby is always fussing about breakages as it is. What he'd say if we began to throw lamps about, I *don't* know."

FOTHERINGAY: "Of course, if I was sure I was always going to have the gift I'd go on the Halls—straight away. I've been thinking of that."

BILL STOKER: "I wouldn't."

ADA: "What would *you* do, Mr. Stoker?"

BILL STOKER: "I'd do better than that."

FOTHERINGAY: "How?"

BILL STOKER: "You tell rabbits to come and violets to come and complexions to come and all that. You're like the Spirit of Nature, Fotheringay. But all that's small beer. What's to prevent you saying: 'Here, let's have a thousand pounds in my pocket? Or for the matter of that, let's have twenty thousand in the bank. And a motor car say—and a big house'."

HOUSEKEEPER: "But is it honest to do things like that?"

FOTHERINGAY: "Maybe there's a limit. Of course, it would be pleasant-like to have that money in the bank. I'll think of that."

MISS HOOPER: "But don't forget your gift of healing."

24

BILL STOKER: "He could have a miraculous hospital. What's to prevent him? He could start miraculous hospitals all over the place. Just go and clean up everybody once a week. It needn't stand in the way of the other things. And how about a miraculous tip or so for the Derby? Lord, if *I* had it, I'd launch out. I wouldn't go on honouring Grigsby and Blott with my services much longer."

HOUSEKEEPER: "Fair doos, Mr. Stoker. You'd have to give your month's notice."

ADA, with ambition and wild surmise in her eyes. She is seeing Fotheringay in a new light. "The things you might do. You could be rich. You could do anything you liked. You could give presents right and left. Why! you might go into Society, Mr. Fotheringay. You might meet all the celebrated people. You might go to court and see the King!"

BILL STOKER: "Music halls, indeed!"

FOTHERINGAY: "I didn't mean to let all this out so soon. I tell you I'm a bit afraid of it. I don't mean to do anything very much yet."

MISS HOOPER, with a slight flavour of antagonism to Ada: "You listen to me, Mr. Fotheringay. Don't you do anything *rash*. You didn't ought to go about doing miracles just anyhow. You oughtn't to turn your gifts to selfish ends."

BILL STOKER: "Oooh! Here's Uplift."

MISS HOOPER: "Yes, I mean it, Mr. Stoker. This gift of miracles and healing is something very serious. You ought to have advice about it, Mr. Fotheringay."

HOUSEKEEPER: "That's plain sense. You ought to have advice."

FOTHERINGAY scratching his cheek: "I suppose I ought. I didn't think of that."

MISS HOOPER: "There's Mr. Maydig, the new Baptist minister."

HOUSEKEEPER: "No, Mr. Fotheringay ought to go to the Vicar."

BILL STOKER: "And a nice mess they'll make of it for you—either of them. Righteous old buffers without any imagination—leastways the Vicar is. And Maydig's just a spouter. You take my advice, Fotheringay, and do yourself well. Don't give your gift away to anybody."

ADA: "There isn't a woman in the world who wouldn't love to have a man work miracles for her."

Fotheringay glances at her.

MISS HOOPER: "You take advice, Mr. Fotheringay."

HOUSEKEEPER: "Will you collect the plates, Jane. There's rhubarb and custard or bread and butter pudding. Miracles or no miracles, we've got to get on; we can't sit here and keep the shop waiting."

Scene: The Manchester Department in Messrs. Grigsby and Blott's establishment at the end of a busy day. Nothing has been tidied up. There is a stack of goods at one end of the counter in a very disorganised state and there is unrolled and unfolded material upon the counter in great confusion. Fotheringay leans against the fixtures in a profound meditation, picking his teeth.

Enter to him Major Grigsby, boss of Grigsby and Blott: Fotheringay starts to attention, so to speak.

GRIGSBY: "Come, come, Mr. Fotheringay. What's the

matter with you to-day? Here we are five minutes from closing time and look at it—look at it. It's in a hay. You've got half an hour of tidying before you."

FOTHERINGAY: "Sorry, sir. I've had a little worry to-day. But I won't be long." Makes as if to roll up a bit of material and then is struck by a thought.

He makes his characteristic gesture and speaks almost inaudibly: "Apple-pie order."

In an instant rolls roll up, goods fold themselves, stacks of goods straighten up and everything leaps to its place.

Grigsby is amazed. He stands agape. He and Fotheringay confront each other, Fotheringay with his hands on the counter.

FOTHERINGAY to ease the pause: "I said it wouldn't take long, sir."

"No. It *hasn't* taken long. I couldn't follow you. Queer—but—. Very, very queer. You're quite sure, Mr. Fotheringay, that this sort of thing doesn't damage the goods?"

FOTHERINGAY: "Does 'em good, sir."

Grigsby walks slowly across the scene still very dazed. He turns and looks at Fotheringay, who affects to be staring out of the department. Grigsby looks away and then turns again. Mutual scrutiny of two perplexed men. Exit Grigsby sideways with his eyes on Fotheringay. Dissolve on Fotheringay scratching his cheek.

PART VI

The Affair of Mr. Winch

EVENING. The Street. The Long Dragon in the distance. Passers-by. Fotheringay is taking the air after the day's work. He carries a walking-stick. He walks towards the Long Dragon twirling his stick. Becomes irresolute. The twirling of his stick reflects his doubts. Stops and stands still, swings round on one leg and goes off in another direction. No close-up of this. It is all shot at a distance of about 30 yards.

Late evening. Bright moonlight. A stile by the roadside. Fotheringay is discovered sitting on the stile. His expression is exalted; his eyes very wide open. He is halfway between inspiration and idiocy.

FOTHERINGAY: "I can do anything. I can do practically anything. If I wanted to do anything to that old moon I could do it. All the saints and the science that ever was; it's nothing to what I can do. Who's afraid, I tell you. Who's afraid?"

He whacks the stile with his stick and breaks it. "Gaw! I broke my stick and it cost seven-and-six at Christmas. My favourite stick."

FOTHERINGAY addresses his stick pityingly: "Ah, *did* they? But wait a bit, old fellow—wait a bit. How about Master's gift of healing. We'll put that all right and better. 'Ere, be—not a stick but a tree—a rose tree, a great big rose tree, right there on the footpath—all covered with lovely roses—and get your breath."

FOTHERINGAY: "Hullo, who's that coming along the road? Old Bobby Winch. This won't do. Go back, I tell you. Lord!"

The rose tree recedes rapidly and hits Winch, one of the local police force, who is just looking round a bit, violently. He has just come in sight down the road. For a time Winch is seen in a sort of Laocoön conflict with a much too floriferous and thorny and abundant crimson-rambler rose.

FOTHERINGAY: "Gollys! Leave him alone! Come off it! Let that rose tree vanish."

The rose tree vanishes.

Winch advances upon Fotheringay, who slides down off his stile and confronts him. Winch's helmet is disarranged. His face is abundantly scratched and his expression formidable.

WINCH: "Hullo, Mister. What's the game? What's this throwing about of brambles, eh?"

FOTHERINGAY: "I wasn't throwing any brambles. Fact is—well, what I was doing was just a bit of a miracle like."

WINCH: "Ooohoo! It's you, Mr. Miracle Worker. It's you, is it? This is how you spend your nights, eh? Just practising another one, eh? Well, this time you've done one trick too many. You've got yourself into real trouble."

FOTHERINGAY: "I didn't mean that bush to hurt you, Mr. Winch. I really didn't."

29

WINCH: "Well, you did. You've assaulted the police in the execution of their duty. From all I hear you've been making yourself a public nuisance for some time. *Now* you've done it."

FOTHERINGAY: "Well—but. It's easy explained."

WINCH: "I'm glad of that because you'll have a fair chance to explain it to the Superintendent."

FOTHERINGAY: "But, Mr. Winch, you don't mean to say you're going to take it seriously like that."

WINCH: "It isn't me takes it seriously; it's the Law."

FOTHERINGAY almost tearful: "What, run me in! Me —so respectable. You can't do it, Mr. Winch."

WINCH: "I'm doing it now. Come along."

FOTHERINGAY: "I won't come."

WINCH: "You will."

FOTHERINGAY: "Oh, go to Hades! Why, I—"

FOTHERINGAY stops aghast. The policeman has vanished.

"Here! Gollys! He's gone." Fotheringay's face is more like a pale moon than ever. Whispers: "He's gone . . . gone . . . to . . . Hades!"

FOTHERINGAY: "If I bring him back he'll tell everyone. . . ."

Dissolve to a desolate place under a lurid light among rocks. Thin wisps of vapour rise from the soil. A strange, half-animal vegetation maintains a precarious hold on the rocks. Two grave phantoms in togas pass across the scene, conversing profoundly. They are unsubstantial and nearly transparent. Constable Winch appears abruptly, legs wide apart and amazed.

THE AFFAIR OF MR. WINCH

"Where *am* I?" Pushes helmet back and scratches his head.

WINCH: "He's got me into some sort of pitfall. There's no end to his tricks. It's—warm here. Hullo!" Small lizard-like creature runs across the foreground. Something flaps across overhead, but only its shadow is seen on the rocks.

Winch is evidently becoming frightened, but he bears up bravely. He takes out his notebook. "I'd better make a note of some of this." Produces stump of a pencil. "The young constable should always make a careful note. Now what was the exact time?" Consults wrist watch. "Why, the paper's going brown. Hot on the boots too. Phew!"

Scene flashes back to Fotheringay standing in the empty moonlit road.

FOTHERINGAY: "Hades? That can't be a nice place. I can't send a chap to Hades like that. Wonder where my little old stick is. Oh—let my stick come back here now—no, not broken. And now what am I to do about Winch?"

FOTHERINGAY appeals to the night: "What am I to do about Winch?"

FOTHERINGAY: "He can't come back. I can't have him staying—there . . . *I* know! San Francisco! That's half round the world—nearly. Let Mr. Winch, wherever he is, go immediately to San Francisco. And—"

Instantaneous flash to a busy street in San Francisco.

All this scene is to be bright and clear and rather small. It is to have something of the effect of a scene watched through field-glasses at some distance. No

31

voices. The music is of horns and buzzers and shouts, but very small like the horns of fairyland. (N.B. Since it is 12.30 A.M. in Essex, it is 4.30 P.M. in San Francisco.)

Just at the climax of a traffic stop Mr. Winch, notebook and pencil in hand and helmet rather askew, appears abruptly. Traffic is released. Disorganisation of traffic by an unexpected obstacle. Marvellous escapes of Mr. Winch. His own movements are precipitate, ill-advised but singularly fortunate. Pursued by two San Francisco cops and an irritated crowd he reaches the side-walk. There he makes a valiant attempt to run for it, knocks over a Chinese laundryman, upsets an apple-basket, gets a little way up a ladder and is caught by a cop and is lost sight of in a great and growing crowd of spectators.

Return to Mr. Fotheringay walking slowly homeward.

"I got to have advice. I certainly got to have advice. What I ought to do about 'im ultimately I *don't* know. Extraordinary power it is. If I remember to send him back every two or three days like, that ought to be all right. But it isn't only Winch. No. And there's all these other ideas I keep on having—all these different ideas. Some of the things I'm beginning to think of—they frighten me. . . ."

"Yet I might do them. Try them anyhow."

"That about Ada."

A smiling expression shows the onset of an agreeable reverie.

"Take the shine out of Mr. Billy Stoker."

PART VIa

Love Interlude

THE same moonlit night. A lane between overhanging high hedges, beneath which everything is very dim, emerges upon a clearer space as it debouches on the road. Two dark forms are seen bending together as they come down the lane discreetly. Their movements suggest participated guilt. As they emerge into the moonlight they are seen to be Ada and Billy Stoker.

ADA: "Well now, Bill, you can't say I don't love you any more."

BILL: "You're a darling, Ada. A perfect darling. *My* darling."

ADA: "*Your* darling really?"

BILL: "Really." He takes her in his arms and kisses her.

ADA, with a deep sigh: "It's lovely. It's heaven. Being like this. And to think you was jealous, Bill, of that poor little Fotheringay!"

BILL: "Him and his miracles!"

ADA: "It must be awful late, Bill."

BILL: "Gollys! past the half hour. Time we was indoors. Door will be locked. Have to ring."

ADA: "We can't go back together, Bill. Everyone would talk."

BILL: "Yes." He considers the situation. "You go back to the front door. And I'll go round the back and shin up the waterpipe to the men's dormitory. I've done it before. The window's never fastened. I'll go off—round the lane, the lane you know."

ADA: "Don't fall down."

BILL: "Not me."

ADA: "Give us a last kiss, Bill."

The picture dissolves while they are still kissing.

Ada is seen walking demurely along the street towards the audience and towards the establishment of Messrs. Grigsby and Blott. At a street corner there enters from the left MR. FOTHERINGAY, deep in a lover's meditation.

"Why, Ada! The very girl I was thinking of!"

ADA: "Why, it's George! D'you know the time, George? It's nice to be you and live out and not have to be in by half past ten every night."

FOTHERINGAY, stopping before her: "I could stay out all night in moonlight like this, Ada. Couldn't you?"

ADA: "It's lovely. Yes, it's real lovely. Done any more miracles, George?"

FOTHERINGAY: "Well—nothing to speak of. Not much fun doing miracles alone. One wants an inspiration. F'r instance. Here—. See the church clock?"

They both look round. The church clock is seen showing a quarter to eleven.

FOTHERINGAY'S voice: "Here, you—and every clock and watch in Dewhinton, go back twenty minutes—twenty-five minutes—*now!*"

The clock goes back.

34

Return to the street.

FOTHERINGAY is seen showing his wrist-watch to Ada by the light of a match. "See? My watch too! You're all right, Ada. If you have to ring and be let in, the hall clock will bear you out."

ADA: "That's what I call a Real Miracle, George. And a very nice one."

FOTHERINGAY: "It's nothing to what I *could* do—for *you,* Ada. D'you know why I made it twenty-five minutes instead of twenty? Just to have a bit of a word with *you,* Ada. See?"

A coquettish: "Well, you *deserve* five minutes, George."

FOTHERINGAY: "I deserve a lot more than that. I'd do—oh, I'd do extraordinary things for you, Ada. You seem to stir up my imagination."

ADA: "It's very kind what you *have* done."

FOTHERINGAY: "Oh, Ada. I'd do anything—if I could get you to sort of love me. Indeed I would. If I could get you—so's you wanted to kiss me."

ADA: "Oh, George! Miracles or no miracles, you mustn't talk to me like that."

FOTHERINGAY: "Why shouldn't I? Don't you care for me? Not a little bit?"

ADA: "Not in *that* way. No . . ." (She deliberately drops the George.) "Mr. Fotheringay."

FOTHERINGAY: "Why not?"

ADA: "I don't know. I just don't."

FOTHERINGAY: "Anyone else, Ada? Eh? *I* know."

ADA: "That's not your business, Mr. Fotheringay. Anyhow, I don't care for you like that. Not in that way.

You're a nice chap but not *my* sort of chap. It isn't your fault, or my fault, or anybody's fault. If there is any-one or no one it wouldn't make any difference about us. I couldn't love you."

FOTHERINGAY: "No?"

ADA: "No. And that's that."

FOTHERINGAY: "Here, wait a bit, Ada! Hold on! Are you so sure you're never going to love me? How about a miracle? How about making you?"

ADA: "You couldn't do that, Mr. Fotheringay." (Frightened, she recoils.) "You *wouldn't* do that, Mr. Fotheringay."

FOTHERINGAY: "Oh! Now, let me see, my lady. Let's see what we can do. *Won't* I do it! Here, now—you be in love with me. You be hopelessly in love with me now. Forget all about Bill Stoker and be in love with me. *Now.*"

She stares at him fascinated. For a moment she says nothing. Then she whispers: *"No."* (Then, louder.) "No." (Then aloud, exultantly.) *"No.* No, I'm not a bit more in love with you than I was. It doesn't work. It doesn't work, Mr. Fotheringay. No, I'm not changed a bit about you. You and your tricks. I'm not an old clock or a rabbit or anything like that. But you fright- ened me, Mr. Fotheringay. Oh! You *did* frighten me." She looks at him, still a bit afraid. "Time I was in, Mr. Fotheringay." She turns and runs off. "Goodnight."

PART VII

Business Opportunity

MAJOR GRIGSBY in his inner sanctum in the establishment of Grigsby and Blott. The Major is a self-important, shortish man of the military shop-walker type.
His sanctum is separated by a glass partition from the
counting-house beyond which is a glimpse of the general shop. Papers and patterns and one lady's hat on a
stand adorn the large desk at which the Major is sitting.
The Major is thinking out what he has to say to Fotheringay. He rehearses phrases in dumb show. Finally
touches a bell on his desk. Small boy apprentice appears. "Send Fotheringay to me. No—no. Ask Mr. Fotheringay to come to see me."

Rehearses more than ever. Gets up and walks up and
down the little office—in silent argument.

FOTHERINGAY appears, or at least his forehead and nose
appear, above the frosted part of the glass pane of the
door of the sanctum. Habit makes him defer to Grigsby
but there is a growing self-confidence in his manner.
He surveys the Major and the Major surveys him. He
opens the door slowly and says with a politeness that
is not in the least abject: "You wished to see me, sir?"

Grigsby, in true shop-walker fashion, places the second office-chair for him. Then, recalling their respective stations, he walks round his desk.

GRIGSBY takes his seat at the desk: "Sit down, Mr. Fotheringay, I want a talk with you." Fotheringay takes the other chair.

Grigsby at his desk becomes the great business organiser; the man of penetration and character. Fotheringay is, as usual, uncertain about himself, distracted between his new sense of power and his old sense of inferiority. He is typically the human being with a gift.

GRIGSBY: "Well, yes. I want a talk with you. Fact is— Mr. Fotheringay, I couldn't help being struck by the way you tidied up your department last night. Very much struck. Practically instantaneous. Could you—ah— could you" (Head on one side) "—tell me in any way how you managed it? I'm told it isn't the only thing of that sort you have done."

FOTHERINGAY is vaguely on his guard—he hardly knows against what. "I could tell you—and, so to speak, I couldn't. I suppose, roughly, it's what one might call a miracle."

GRIGSBY: "Isn't that rather an old-fashioned word, Miracle?"

FOTHERINGAY: "Well, suppose one said it was something—something contrariwise to the course of nature done by an act of will."

GRIGSBY: "Ah, *will*. Now there is something I can understand. A man doesn't build up a big and vital business like this—with three branches already and forty-nine assistants—out of one small shop with five hands, in seven short years, without knowing something of Will

Power. Will Power over assistants, over partners, over customers. . . . But frankly, Mr. Fotheringay, you haven't struck me as the kind of young man who went in for that sort of thing."

FOTHERINGAY: "I haven't. It's just come to me."

GRIGSBY: "You never studied Dominance—never exercised your will against other wills?"

FOTHERINGAY: "Only occasionally, I suppose, with customers."

GRIGSBY: "And that not very successfully."

FOTHERINGAY: "Even now I don't seem able to do much with that. It's miracles—well, just old-fashioned miracles I do—like magic, bit of healing and that style of stuff, making things and animals appear and disappear; moving things and people about like from here to there. Changing things. That it seems I can do practically without limit. I never knew it before—but I can."

GRIGSBY beginning to concentrate on him and pointing a compelling finger: "But not to get down to feelings and motives?"

FOTHERINGAY: "No, I don't seem able to do that."

GRIGSBY: "Have you tried?"

FOTHERINGAY evasively: "It wasn't much good."

GRIGSBY: "But tell me—tell me."

FOTHERINGAY: "It was only that I wanted someone to feel differently about me. It wasn't anything. Never mind about that."

GRIGSBY: "Lady in the case? Well, we won't talk about that. Nothing in that direction—no. Coming down to solid fact, Mr. Fotheringay, I want to make you a business proposition. Now. Now—. I take it that even if you

can't absolutely *make* 'em want to come in and buy,
you can offer inducements—considerable inducements.
Efficiency. Service. F'r instance, you could straighten
up our shops, open them in the morning, deliver our
parcels to the addresses given . . . All by miracle, eh?
Have you thought of that, eh? Why not? I've been
thinking of the way you straightened up that department last night. I do that at times. Think things out in
the small hours. My mental life—few people suspect it.
Intense concentration. Now, here we are! Grigsby, Blott
and Fotheringay, the Miracle Drapers. Naturally you
contract to confine your gift entirely to our organisation. No outside miracles. Do you get me, Mr. Fotheringay?"

FOTHERINGAY: "Yes, but—"

GRIGSBY: "I've figured it out. I've figured it out in my
head. We could guarantee you, sir, an income of £3,000
in the first year—three thousand pounds! There isn't a
competitor we couldn't down by sheer rapidity and
economy. We could extend over the west coast, over
England. There's no limit with an advantage like that.
Call me a dreamer, Mr. Fotheringay. I tell you every
great business organiser is a dreamer. The Poetry of
Commerce! But I can see Grigsby, Blott and Fotheringay now, from this chair, running into millions of capi-
tal and spreading all round the world."

FOTHERINGAY: "All round the world, eh?"

GRIGSBY: "All round the world!"

FOTHERINGAY, deep in thought for a moment: "I suppose, sir, San Francisco *is* pretty near all round the
world, isn't it?"

40

GRIGSBY: "Practically so—essentially so. Why?"

FOTHERINGAY: "Thought struck me. I suppose you don't know, sir, how long it takes to get here from San Francisco?"

GRIGSBY: "Three weeks or a month I should think. Why do you ask?"

FOTHERINGAY: "Three weeks anyhow?"

GRIGSBY: "*All* that. Why do you ask?"

FOTHERINGAY: "I just wanted to know. I've got a sort of relation there."

Flash to a brief bright scene in a San Francisco hospital. Mr. Winch's clothes, belt and helmet are seen hanging on a peg or in a cupboard, and being scrutinised by the typical gangster reporter (Y) of the films. To him comes another more intelligent type (X below). (The reporters who speak are X, Y, Z.) The picture comes round to Mr. Winch with a bandaged head sitting in a wheeled chair surrounded by baffled (typical) newspaper-men.

X: "And that's all you've got to tell us, Mr. Winch?"

WINCH: "That's all I got to tell you."

Y: "Wal—it's Crazy."

Z: "It don't *begin* to make sense."

Winch goes out of the picture which comes to a conversational close-up of the reporters. There is one man, X, with a finer mind than the others and he is most impressed by the whole affair.

Y: "You can't make a story of that, boys—he's screwy."

Z: "What's all the dope about roses and brambles—anyhow?"

X: "These clothes he's got are the real genuine Eng-

41

lish cop's uniform. I tell you there's something in it. Fourth Dimension, or something."

Y: "Where'd he scram from? That's the only thing in it that interests *me*."

X: "How about the clothes?"

Z: "Aw, to hell with the clothes! The Ed won't print a line of the stuff. We can have people *disappearing* all over the United States. That's fair copy; that is. But this chap suddenly *appearing*. You can't stuff 'em with that."

X: "There's his clothes I tell you—and his poor little toasted note-book."

Z: "And notes you can't read!"

X: "But it's true. He's a genuine English cop and he's come straight from Essex here. In a flash. *How?* Lord knows. But he came so fast, his shoes and his book were frizzled."

Y: "Might make it a case of materialisation."

Z: "You try that on the mugs who read your sheet. I wanna keep my job."

Y: "Yes—kid 'em with it."

X: "This news racket is plain nuts. We're supposed to be always looking for something new. Well, here's something new—something that's never happened before. And because we can't fit it in on any of the stock stories—we've got to cut it out. We've got to cut it out, boys. Just as we should have had to cut out a story about flying or submarines or radio—fifty years ago. It's *new news* and the truth is you mustn't have new news in a newspaper. Wod! Wod! Of all the mean and feeble things that ever crawled on its belly in the mud, the human imagination is the meanest and feeblest! Here's the most wonderful and unaccountable thing that has ever happened—and we can't spill it. . . ."

x reflects indignantly: "I'll make the front page with this yarn—or pass out. I'll bring imagination to bear on it somehow." Protesting face comes close up. "Can't they tell the Wonderful when they see it? Are they *never* to be taken out of their mean little selves?"

Dissolve back to Major Grigsby talking to Fotheringay, who is not so much excited and convinced as being dragged along by the Major's compelling flow.

GRIGSBY: "You must bring imagination to bear on this. If you let this gift of yours just splash about—you'll waste it. It will do no good to you or anyone. Miracle here. Miracle there. Just scattering miracles. Cheap as dirt. But canalised—concentrated! Monopolised! Limited strictly to the expansion of Grigsby, Blott and Fotheringay, this can be an immense thing!"

FOTHERINGAY: "All this is very *attractive*."

GRIGSBY: "Attractive. It's the logic of the situation. I see us springing up in a night to be giants in the distributing world—big business—big money—big men. Monopolists. We can't miss it. I tell you what, Mr. Fotheringay. I'd like to have the reactions of Mr. Bampfylde to this—Mr. Bampfylde of the bank over the way."

PART VIII

High Finance

FOTHERINGAY, Major Grigsby and Mr. Bampfylde are discovered in a little parlour of the Dewhinton branch of the London and Essex Bank.

Mr. Bampfylde is a small, lean, dry, very "efficient" man, wearing a pince-nez. Grigsby is flushed and dishevelled with his own eloquence in propounding his new and wonderful scheme. Fotheringay seems to have done some thinking while the other two have been talking. By degrees the deference of conscious inferiority is evaporating from his manner. A certain native shrewdness and simplicity is becoming more apparent. And he is beginning to conceive of himself as a potential capitalist of importance. His attitude is easier. He does not "sit-up" as he did in Grigsby's sanctum.

BAMPFYLDE: "It's a most extraordinary proposition, Major Grigsby. If you had told me two hours ago that miracles would be worked in this parlour—and that I should be confronted with a project for a world net of miraculous chain stores I should have scouted the idea —scouted the idea."

GRIGSBY: "And you don't now?"

BAMPFYLDE: "I do not."

GRIGSBY: "It took me a painful night to grasp all this. And get it in order."

BAMPFYLDE: "I shall have trouble with headquarters, but I think I can handle that. Mr. Fotheringay, I think you may count on having the London and Essex Bank behind you. I think you may count on us, Major Grigsby."

FOTHERINGAY: "Ye-es. I suppose this is how it ought to be done. I don't know much about finance and business management myself. But now—what you propose is that I should be sort of exclusive."

GRIGSBY: "Confine your gift entirely to Grigsby, Blott and Fotheringay. That's—*essential.*"

Bampfylde nods endorsement.

FOTHERINGAY: "It's just there I don't *see* it."

Both await his further utterance.

FOTHERINGAY: "Now there's the gift of healing—and that sort of thing. I don't want to make a business of that."

GRIGSBY, brilliant idea: "We could have free clinics in all our stores. Healing, Tuesdays and Fridays—and special bargain lines. Free. Absolutely without charge."

FOTHERINGAY: "Ye-es. We *might* do that. But what I don't see is—why don't we give away all the stuff free? Why make a business of it?"

GRIGSBY: "You can't do that. You positively can't do that."

FOTHERINGAY, yielding: "I suppose you can't. No. And then, why do we have to borrow money for it and —what did you call it?—issue debentures?"

BAMPFYLDE: "You must have the thing put on a sound financial basis."

FOTHERINGAY, trying to grasp it: "We got to make money by it."

GRIGSBY with profundity: "Solvency, sir, is the test of service."

FOTHERINGAY: "But why, if we want money, why not make money right away?"

BAMPFYLDE: "It can't be done." (Pause. Growing alarmed.) "Without quite disastrous results."

FOTHERINGAY: "But look here." (Holds out his hand and his lips move. A hundred pound note appears.)

BAMPFYLDE: "No. No! You can't do that. That's illegal. That's forgery. That note's a forged note."

FOTHERINGAY: "Look at it. All right, isn't it?"

BAMPFYLDE, fingering the note: "Oh, this won't do." (Gets up in his agitation.) "This will NOT do. You mustn't make money when you want it. Strikes at the root of—everything. Puts the whole banking system out of gear. People must *want* money."

GRIGSBY: "And they've got to *want* commodities."

FOTHERINGAY: "But if I can give them all they want!"

GRIGSBY and BAMPFYLDE together: "What would they DO? What incentive would there be for anybody—to do anything?"

FOTHERINGAY, scratching his cheek: "Couldn't they have some fun—like?"

GRIGSBY jumps up. Fotheringay sits perplexed but not protesting actively.

BAMPFYLDE: "I can assure you, Mr. Fotheringay—I can assure you. I have studied these questions—very

46

profound questions—before you were born. Human society, I repeat, is based on want. Life is based on want. Wild-eyed visionaries—I name no names—may dream of a world without need. Cloud-cuckoo-land. It can't be done."

FOTHERINGAY: "It 'asn't been tried, 'as it?"

BAMPFYLDE: "It couldn't be tried."

FOTHERINGAY's face remains sceptical.

GRIGSBY: "You take my word for it, Mr. Fotheringay. You can't go just *heaping* things on people without a *quid pro quo*. It would ruin everything. Universal bankruptcy. Lassitude. Degeneration. Now, if only you will follow us—trust us . . . We have worked out this scheme for—keeping your gift—your very dangerous gift, if I may say so—within bounds. Incidentally *you* will become a multi-millionaire. Not a doubt of it. And people will get what they want—within measure."

BAMPFYLDE: "A general encouraging gradual rise in prosperity. Nothing extravagant. Above all, no violent changes."

FOTHERINGAY: "I got to think it all over."

A shop vista in the establishment of Grigsby and Blott. At the far end the front door and street outside. An assistant serves a customer in the background. Close up. Bill Stoker is floor-walking in the absence of Major Grigsby. He adjusts a display of sunshades. Another assistant stands at the counter.

ASSISTANT: "Where's Fotheringay to-day?"

STOKER: "Haven't seen him all the morning. Governor sent for him."

ASSISTANT: "He's got the swap perhaps."

STOKER: "Likely enough."

ASSISTANT: "All this foolery with miracles!"

STOKER: "Only get him into trouble. *He* can't do anything with it. He's got no imagination. Now if only *I* could snatch it from him." (Twirls a sunshade and kisses his hand.)

Fotheringay appears from street in doorway down vista and advances up shop. A few days ago he would have been deferential to the customer and he would have dodged round behind the counter at once. Now he disregards the customer and marches in a brown study up the middle of the shop. He has a new air of responsibility about him. He looks up as he approaches Bill Stoker, regards him absent-mindedly and then nods.

STOKER: "Hullo Fotheringay, what's up? Where you been all the morning?"

ASSISTANT: "He's got the swap."

FOTHERINGAY shakes his head slowly—smiling slightly. He is fairly self-important but rather anxious to get their reactions to what he has to say. "Not it. I've been considering a business proposition. What do you think of Grigsby, Blott and Fotheringay, Miraculous Stores?"

ASSISTANT: "Oh! Get *out!*"

FOTHERINGAY: "Yes, I got a firm proposal. Big business. I didn't realise it before, but there's a lot of money in these miracles—properly handled. Big money."

STOKER: "Gee! Miraculous stores, eh?"

FOTHERINGAY: "That's about it."

ASSISTANT: "Put us all out of work."

FOTHERINGAY: "Didn't think of that."

STOKER: "You haven't signed on?"

FOTHERINGAY: "No. I sort of feel I ought to think it over."

STOKER: "Who's in it?"

FOTHERINGAY: "Oh, Grigsby—and the Bank."

STOKER: "Yes, but why make money for them? Why not make it for yourself?"

FOTHERINGAY: "I'd make money all right."

STOKER: "Why make it for *them?* If you want money —make it for yourself. Why fatten up old Grigsby and Bampfylde?"

FOTHERINGAY: "You can't do it that way. You can't make money for yourself."

STOKER: "Why not?"

FOTHERINGAY: "Oh! Mr. Bampfylde has explained. He made it very clear. Lead to social chaos. Universal bankruptcy. Break up the social system."

STOKER: "Break up old Grigsby and Blott, you mean."

FOTHERINGAY: "He didn't think it ought to be done."

STOKER: "He'd do it fast enough if he knew how to do it himself. I tell you, Fotheringay, these chaps are just sucking on to you. Gaw, if *I* had your gift—"

FOTHERINGAY: "Well?"

STOKER: "I'd run the world."

Fotheringay looks at him with his head on one side.

STOKER: "What price Bill Stoker's New Deal? I'd make a world of it! I wouldn't put my gift into blinkers and harness it to Grigsby, Blott and Co. No fear!"

Fotheringay's face taking it in. It is a new but assimilable idea.

PART IX

The Transfiguration of Ada Price

THE costume department of Grigsby, Blott and Co. Dress stands with costumes. Mirrors. It is slack time and no customers are present. Miss Ada Price is discovered at a mirror, with her lipstick.

Fotheringay enters and stands regarding her. Mutual hesitation because of the overnight scene.

ADA with affected sangfroid: "Hullo, George."

FOTHERINGAY: "Making yourself prettier than ever, eh?"

ADA: "Wish I needn't do it, George. But it has to be done. Lipstick and powder. Why don't you give me a complexion like you gave to Effie? She's dazzling. Considering all you might do, I think you're pretty mean about your miracles."

FOTHERINGAY, holding it for a bit: "Oh! bless you!"

Inaudible instructions and gesture.

Ada becomes much more beautiful.

ADA, still at the mirror: "Now, that's nice, George. Such a becoming wave in the hair, too. Oh, I like little ME. Poised on a delicate neck! I suppose it won't run to a diamond tiara or anything of the sort?"

FOTHERINGAY: *"Well!* Why not?"

50

THE TRANSFIGURATION OF ADA PRICE

Diamond tiara. Ada puts up her hand, incredulously.

FOTHERINGAY: "Look in the glass."

ADA, starts: "Oh, *lovely!* Why, it might be *real*. It's *wonderful.*"

FOTHERINGAY: "It *is* real."

ADA: "Oh, yes! Could you do a pearl necklace, George, to go with it? How you do it I *don't* know. It's madness!"

Ada is so absorbed with the pearls in the mirror that she almost forgets Fotheringay.

FOTHERINGAY: "And while we're at it. Why wear that old black dress? 'Ere, let her be dressed in splendid robes like Cleopatra in the play."

Transfiguration of Ada Price.

Fotheringay is overwhelmed at the result of his own miracle. Ada stands splendid and triumphant. She doesn't look at Fotheringay. She is exalted by her own effect.

FOTHERINGAY: "Ada, you're wonderful."

ADA: "It's you who are wonderful, Mr. Fotheringay. I never saw anything like it. If Bill could see me now— he'd faint!"

FOTHERINGAY realises with a start that customers are coming into the department. " 'Ere's customers coming. They'll see you like that. 'Ere! Ada, be as you were before I changed you!"

ADA becomes the commonplace young woman she was before. She looks into the mirror: "I've gone back. I've gone back. George, did it ever happen?"

Fotheringay is already picking up his boxes again. The customers enter the department escorted by Bill

Stoker (floor walking) and Ada rouses herself to serve them. She is still rather distraught and queenly in her manner.

Fotheringay hesitates, looks back at her, hesitates again and goes out of the department, profoundly disturbed.

PART X

Taking Advice

THE Assistants' sitting-room at Messrs. Grigsby and Blott. It is a not too well furnished apartment, with a small bookcase, horsehair sofa and chairs, table, etc. A clock indicates a quarter past nine. Miss Maggie Hooper is discovered alone with a basket of needlework.

Enter Fotheringay. He stands regarding her.

MISS HOOPER: "And what are *you* doing in the house at this time of night?"

FOTHERINGAY: "I don't know. I just came in. I think I wanted to see you." (He sits down on the sofa.) "Maggie, there's something frightening about this miracle working."

MISS HOOPER: "I told you to get advice about it."

FOTHERINGAY: "I don't get anything *but* advice about it, but it's all different. I don't know where I am. I'm sort of bursting with wonders and I don't dare let 'em loose. There's things happening *in* me, more miraculous than anything happening outside me. I'm beginning to want things—and think of things. I can't tell you. Maggie, I got a *bad* imagination. I got a *dangerous* imagination."

MISS HOOPER: "Well, what did I tell you? You go and

see Mr. Maydig. You could see him to-night. He gives people advice in his parlour."

FOTHERINGAY: "I wonder what *'E'll* tell me."

MISS HOOPER: "I've asked you to go and hear him preach time after time. He's wonderful when he really gets going. Seems to lift you up. Takes you right out of yourself."

Dissolve to Mr. Maydig in his study.

Mr. Maydig is seated in a low arm-chair by the side of a newly-lit fire. He is a long man, with long arms, legs, wrists and neck. He has the fluting voice of an emotional preacher and the normal expression of his face is one of rapture and exaltation. There is a small table convenient to his elbow on which are a number of books, a *Daily Herald* and a weekly paper, *The New Age,* a bottle of whisky, a syphon and a glass of whisky and soda. The books shown by a momentary close-up are Jean's "Through Space and Time," Temple's "Nature, Man and God," Dunne's "Serial Universe," Weatherhead's "Psychology and Life," and G. D. H. and M. I. Cole's "Guide to Modern Politics."

Mr. Maydig appears to be reading Bertrand Russell's "Freedom and Organisation."

He holds the book in one long hand and gesticulates with the other. He is not so much reading as making his own commentary. Indeed he is hardly reading at all; the book is merely a stimulant.

MAYDIG: "Ah—ah! Wonderful, wonderful. 'To take this sorry scheme of things entire and mould it better to the heart's desire.' Yes, my dear friends, my dearly beloved friends, this poor disordered world, this rich and marvellous world. Do you ever . . . No! Do we ever—No, no, no. When do we ever lift up our eyes from the things—the sordid urgent little things about us—think—dream—dream of what the world might be? Not bad that;—Dream of what the world might be. If only we had the power—if only we had the faith to do that . . ."

There is a knock at the door and his housekeeper appears.

"There's a young man, sir, very anxious to see you. Name of Fotheringay. Says it's urgent."

MAYDIG considers: "Fotheringay?—Don't know him. Respectable? Not—a mendicant?"

HOUSEKEEPER: "Nothing of that sort. But he's in some trouble, sir, says he wants advice."

MAYDIG: "Show him in then—show him in. I never refuse myself—if it's like that. Always ready to give what I *can* give."

The housekeeper goes out and Maydig puts whisky, syphon, etc., out of sight, after a hasty drink at the whisky. Rearranges books to make their titles more evident. Stands on hearthrug to receive his visitor. Raises himself on his toes. Looms impressively. Enter Fotheringay rather diffidently.

MAYDIG: "Well, sir, what can I do for you?"

FOTHERINGAY: "I'm told you sometimes give good advice to people—and I've got a peculiar sort of trouble—if you can call it a trouble—which perhaps a minister like yourself—"

MAYDIG: "Go on."

FOTHERINGAY: "Well, something very extraordinary has happened to me. I used to think I couldn't do anything. Now—I begin to find I can do just whatever I want to do—by will power."

MAYDIG: "What do you mean, will power?"

FOTHERINGAY: "Work miracles."

MAYDIG: "Miracles!"

FOTHERINGAY: "Ye-eah, miracles—no end of them!"

MAYDIG regards his caller profoundly. "My dear sir—are you by any chance mad? There are no such things as miracles under the present dispensation, I can assure you."

FOTHERINGAY: "Would you think differently—if I worked one?"

MAYDIG: "Well—I'd think it over. I have an open mind. Nobody can deny me that."

FOTHERINGAY: " 'Ere goes—what shall it be? Make something appear, eh? Oh! I'm sick of messing about with rabbits and kittens and bunches of flowers. 'Ere! let there be a panther 'ere—a *real* panther—on the hearthrug."

A panther appears crouching between the two men. Maydig starts back and upsets his little table. Fotheringay is evidently also alarmed at the quality of the animal produced. The beast itself is as frightened as either of them. It is on the defensive. It crouches close to the floor and turns its head from one to the other snarling dangerously; then it leaps forward and swings round so as to face them both with its back to the audience, filling up the greater part of the picture.

The voice of FOTHERINGAY is heard: " 'Ere! Vanish. Cease to exist."

56

TAKING ADVICE

The panther vanishes and Maydig and Fotheringay confront each other across a crumpled hearthrug.

FOTHERINGAY: "How's that for a miracle?"

MAYDIG recovering slowly: "Something wonderful—yes. A miracle, no!"

FOTHERINGAY: "You mean—there wasn't a real panther 'ere a minute ago?"

MAYDIG: "No, my dear sir. No. Joint hallucination. The thing is quite well known."

FOTHERINGAY: "That panther was an hallucination! 'Ere! I'll bring it back."

MAYDIG: "No! don't do that. But—"

FOTHERINGAY: "Look at these paw marks on the floor. See? Hallucinations don't leave footsteps like that, do they?"

MAYDIG: "I'm willing to be convinced. Yes—yes. There *are* paw marks. Some large carnivore." (His last resistances vanish.) "And you find you really can do things like that? You know Mr.—Mr.—"

FOTHERINGAY: "Fotheringay."

MAYDIG: "Mr. Fotheringay, that was a miracle you did just now. You needn't have any further doubts about it. It was a miracle. Can you do—many other things—of the same sort?"

FOTHERINGAY: "That's what I want to consult you about, Mr. Maydig. I can do all sorts of things. I can heal people. I can clear things up and set things right. I can change things into other things. I can move things about. I don't seem able to get into the insides of people's minds, so to speak, but except for that there doesn't seem to be a limit—not a limit to what I can do."

MAYDIG, head on one side—dreaming expression—grasping the facts. "It's Power."

FOTHERINGAY: "Yes. But what am I going to *do* about it? What would you do about it if you were me? What would *anyone* do? You know, Mr. Maydig, it's a most remarkable thing, before I knew I could work miracles I thought I knew everything I wanted—and wasn't going to get it. And now I can, in a manner of speaking, have everything—something seems to hold me back." He leaves off, doubtful if Maydig is listening.

MAYDIG still getting hold of the vast idea: "Power. Pow-er. My dear young man, what might you not do—what may you not do with the world? Healing! Have you thought?"

He lays a bony hand on Fotheringay's shoulder and points the lone forefinger of the other at vacancy. "Why not banish disease from the world? Do in one swoop, what science and medicine have been toiling to do little by little! A world without disease."

FOTHERINGAY: "I hadn't thought of that. I thought I'd just go about and cure somebody here and somebody there."

MAYDIG: "Sweep it *all* away. A world glowing with health—newborn.

"The world's great age begins anew.

"The golden years return.

"The earth doth like a snake renew her winter weeds outworn. And then peace! You can give them plenty—make corn, power yield a thousandfold. What is there left to fight about?"

FOTHERINGAY: "You don't think there may be a catch in it somewhere?"

MAYDIG: "What catch?"

FOTHERINGAY: "I think I'd rather go gradually for a bit. When you get on the big side—it's unexpected sometimes. That panther—"

MAYDIG with upturned face: "No doubt a certain wise caution is needed, yes. We must go circumspectly. We must harness our panthers. But if we go without haste, let us also go without delay. I see such splendour in this Power of yours, such hope for our race, such starry Hope."

FOTHERINGAY: "Talking of upsetting things, Major Grigsby and Mr. Bampfylde were very anxious I shouldn't upset things. They did seem to think there might be a catch."

MAYDIG: "Those men have limited minds—extremely limited minds. I have never been able to work with either of them."

FOTHERINGAY sticking to his subject: "You see, what Mr. Bampfylde said was that all human beings are held together by money really and by wanting money and things, and that if they didn't want they wouldn't have anything to do."

MAYDIG: "I find that intolerable. I find that absolutely intolerable. Have they no faith in Man?" He hovers over Fotheringay, enforcing his remarks with gestures of his hands. "Is there no art? Is there no beauty? Are there not boundless seas of knowledge yet unplumbed?"

FOTHERINGAY: "Mr. Bampfylde didn't seem to think

they were likely to go in for that sort of thing all at once."

MAYDIG: "Because the man has no imagination. Because he has no soul. Because he has forgotten the clouds of glory he trailed from heaven in his infancy. The business man! The banker! Save me from them! Man bankrupt—in a world of plenty!"

FOTHERINGAY: "I suppose reely, they *ought* to find a better way of managing things."

MAYDIG: "Of course! But will they ever trouble to do so—until they are compelled? Until things overtake them? No, sir. And that is where we begin. To-morrow. Suppose now—every poor soul in the world found a five-pound note or its equivalent in hand—suddenly. So that they could go out and buy things! Just think of that! Just think of the effect of it."

FOTHERINGAY: "I'd like to do that. If you're sure there's no catch in it. But it will give Mr. Bampfylde fits."

MAYDIG: "Convulsions, I hope—convulsions! And then —healing. All over the world. Everyone suddenly saying 'Ha! Ha! I feel well. I feel strong.' "

FOTHERINGAY: "I don't see any harm in that."

MAYDIG: "Nor I."

FOTHERINGAY: "It might put the doctors out a bit."

MAYDIG: "And why?"

FOTHERINGAY: "Naturally they think it *their* business to keep us healthy—"

MAYDIG: "Oh Heaven! Oh Spirit of Righteousness! Are we to remain needy to please the bankers and business men, and unhealthy to provide fees for the doctors?"

FOTHERINGAY: "I only thought it made things a bit complicated."

MAYDIG: "Well, well. Sleep on it first. We shall have to provide for the doctors and traders—yes, I admit that. It cannot all be done in a flash. There's an inertia in things that has to be considered. I will think and think and think. I shan't sleep, Mr. Fotheringay. Not a wink. I shall keep vigil. The last night of human misery! The pause before the Dawn. What a glorious thought. Will *you* be able to sleep?"

FOTHERINGAY: "Well, I've had a pretty busy day."

MAYDIG: "You are one of God's innocents. You will sleep. And yet I can hardly bear to part like this. Let us do *one simple* good thing before we go to bed to-night —an earnest of all we mean to do. Now let us think. Some little thing. Ah! There is my neighbour here, Colonel Winstanley. Chairman of the Bench—full of influence and all that influence against progress. Always treated me with the utmost incivility. I bear him no malice. He sits late at night and drinks—drinks, I fear, too much. I am no pedant in these matters, but *he*—boozes. He will be sitting now, with his decanter beside him. Change it to some simple non-intoxicating fluid. And all his house is decorated with swords and weapons. Beat them into plough-shares. Turn his swords to reaping-hooks."

FOTHERINGAY: "But will he like it?"

MAYDIG: "Not at first. But it will set him thinking."

FOTHERINGAY, a little reluctantly: "Well, I would like to do something before I turn in. Colonel Winstanley, you said? 'Ere goes." Gesture and inaudible command.

PART X1

The Pacification of Colonel Winstanley

THE hall of the house of Colonel Winstanley. It is decorated with the heads of two tigers and a number of spearheads, kreeses, swords and similar weapons. A bell is heard ringing in gusts. An anxious-looking butler without a tie, buttoning up a coat he has just put on, hurries across the hall. The camera follows him across a large dark conventional drawing-room to the study of the colonel. The colonel is revealed in a mess-jacket standing before an arm-chair beside an open fire with a glass of whisky in his hand and an expression of strong distaste on his face. He is a fine good-looking old soldier, but choler and intolerance are in his blood. He sips and eyes his butler accusingly.

BUTLER: "You rang, sir?"

COLONEL: "I rang six times. You go to bed too soon, Moody. And now, tell me; what the *devil's* the matter with this whisky? It's gone wrong. It's lost its taste. It's flat. It's worse than flat. It's mawkish, I tell you—mawkish. What have you been doing to it? Have you been watering it, Moody? It isn't even whisky!"

BUTLER: "It's the real old stuff, sir. Out of the old jar."

62

COLONEL: "It's *not* the real old stuff, and it's *not* out of the old jar. It's got no fire. It's got no guts. What have you been doing to it?"

BUTLER: "I can assure you, sir—"

COLONEL: "Do you mean to assure me I'm drinking whisky when I know I'm not!"

A frightful clatter of metal falling interrupts the conversation.

COLONEL: "What the devil is *that?* What's happening? First I get water instead of whisky and next the house falls down. Something has happened to the collection. Go and see, man. Go and see. Don't stand staring there."

Exit butler.

The COLONEL returns to his whisky. "It's POISON. I'm being poisoned! Pah! Moody, there! What's happened out there? Why don't you come and tell me?"

The butler's footsteps heard hurrying through drawing-room.

Re-enter butler, leaving the drawing-room door open. His expression is one of horror and amazement and he carries a sickle in his hand.

He speaks slowly: "I don't understand, sir. When I crossed the hall three minutes ago everything seemed as right as could be. And now—it's frightful."

COLONEL: "What's frightful? Speak up, man, what's frightful?"

BUTLER: "The collection, sir—the whole collection."

COLONEL: "Go on, go on!"

BUTLER: "The collection, practically all the collection —well—it's gone, sir."

COLONEL: *"Gone!"*

BUTLER: "Yessir, all the swords have gone—the whole collection, and there's a lot of other things—look like agricultural implements to me, sir—mostly on the floor. This, sir, for example."

Butler holds out a sickle with manifest distaste and the Colonel takes and examines it.

COLONEL in a tone of wonder: "What's this—this blinking Bolshevik thing? What *is* it? What does it mean? Is the house going mad? My swords gone! Gone? What are you saying? I don't understand. Let's have a look at 'em."

Scene changes to hall of the Colonel's house. Colonel and butler survey a scene of wreckage. The Colonel's collection has undergone a complete transformation into plough-shares and reaping-hooks, and most of it is littered on the floor.

After a speechless moment the COLONEL shouts: "If I could lay my hands on the FOOL who did this! Are there no police in Dewhinton? The fellow must have come right in as I was sitting there. He's stolen my swords! I understand that. But what he means by leaving this—this *muck,* beats me."

The outdoor bell rings.

COLONEL: "And who's ringing at this time of night?"

BUTLER: "Can't imagine, sir."

COLONEL: *"Don't* imagine. Go and see! If somebody's trying some sort of game on *me—!"*

Butler opens the outer door. Superintendent Smithells and Constable Thumble appear hesitatingly. The superintendent has a telegram in his hand.

COLONEL, frantic: *"You!* Look at this! Look at this

64

mess here. My swords—my collection. Do you know anything about it? Come in, confound you. Don't stand gaping there on the doorstep. It's just been done. Come in and see what's happened to my weapons!"

The superintendent and constable come in slowly and heavily and stare in perplexity at the litter in the hall. Then they look at each other portentously and deeply.

COLONEL barks: "Well?"

SUPERINTENDENT: "It's some more of it."

COLONEL: "More of *what?*"

SUPERINTENDENT: "These—miracles."

Colonel Winstanley seems on the verge of great eloquence but happily for the censorship finds himself speechless.

SUPERINTENDENT: "There's been a serious outbreak of miracles in the district, sir. Quite beyond anyone's experience."

COLONEL: "Miracles!"

SUPERINTENDENT: "Yessir, miracles."

COLONEL: "There aren't such things."

SUPERINTENDENT: "Not properly, sir. Which makes it so disconcerting, sir. We didn't come disturbing you at this time of night about nothing. But seeing, sir, as you are the Chairman of the Bench, we thought you might be able to help—"

COLONEL: "What is it now? What is it?"

SUPERINTENDENT: "It's about this Constable Winch of ours, what's been missing since last night. We've searched everywhere. We've dragged the millstream. We've made enquiries up and down the railway line."

COLONEL: "You don't expect me to find him for you at ten minutes to midnight, do you?"

SUPERINTENDENT: "No, sir. But we've got a cable."

COLONEL: "What's the good of a cable?"

SUPERINTENDENT: "A telegram, sir—from San Francisco."

COLONEL: "Oh! Is *that* it?" Seizes the telegram. Reads: "Reply paid. 36 words. Police Dewhinton Essex Eng. Is Constable Winch missing stop has appeared mysteriously here stop slightly injured in street riot provoked by himself stop alleged miracle stop accuses one Fotheringay stop any information and instructions for disposal of Constable cable private and exclusive to Will Prackman Office S.F. Stop. All charges to me."

COLONEL: "This is some sort of hoax."

SUPERINTENDENT: "With all due respect, sir, it isn't a hoax. It's something more serious. It's that young fellow, Fotheringay."

COLONEL: "Fotheringay! I must have a whisky. If I can't have a whisky my mind will give way."

BUTLER: "Yessir—but—"

COLONEL: "Good *Lord!* Is that another miracle?"

BUTLER: "I'll get another jar, sir—I'll get one with the seal unbroken."

Shift scene to the Colonel's study. The butler is breaking the seal and uncorking a four-gallon jar of whisky. The others stand round stupefied but still faintly hopeful. Four glasses are filled—neat. There is no trifling with soda-water. Four men taste together and put their glasses down. Their faces are very grave.

COLONEL breaking the silence: "Soap and water."

PACIFICATION OF COLONEL WINSTANLEY

SUPERINTENDENT: "It's nastier than that, sir. I should say it was one of those temperance drinks."

COLONEL: "Well, Moody, anything to say?"

BUTLER: "Sir, I got my weaknesses. But I'd as soon poison a baby as tamper with whisky."

SUPERINTENDENT: "If you ask me—it's Fotheringay again."

COLONEL: "Fotheringay! More Fotheringay. I'll keep calm. I owe it to myself and everyone to keep calm. Oh! perfectly calm. I'll see the fellow to-morrow. No fuss. I'll just talk to him. Quietly. Calmly. No good getting heated. I'll have it out with him. You bring him to me, sort of casually, Smithells. Just for a bit of advice. In my garden. Don't alarm him. . . . And keep your eye on him while you're bringing him. Have your truncheon up your sleeve. If he lifts a finger. If he so much as *looks* like New Zealand or Tokio—*club* him. *I'll* see you through."

The COLONEL reflects: "No, I won't see him to-night. Open air. Open daylight. When you can watch his eyes and hands. One man to another."

PART XII

The Colonel Pleads

THE Colonel's rose-garden. It is an old-fashioned pleasant garden with specimen trees and a monkey-puzzle in
the background. Glimpse of the house. Bright sunshine.
The COLONEL is in white, with a Panama straw hat, and
he carries an instrument for rooting up dandelions and
plantains without stooping. But he is not weeding his
lawn. He paces up and down, weeder behind him. A
sleepless night has done nothing to tranquillise him. He
exhorts himself: "Handle the situation firmly, calmly.
Don't *shout*. Don't get excited. Study your man. Grim
if you like, but no bluster. Ah!"

Superintendent and Fotheringay appear approaching.

COLONEL WINSTANLEY: "So that's the miracle worker,
eh? Don't look it—I must say. Little cad. Spoilt my
whisky, smashed my collection. Don't get excited! The
firm hand! Well, Mr. Superintendent, is this the young
man you wanted me to see?"

SUPERINTENDENT: "This is Mr. Fotheringay, sir—as
directed."

FOTHERINGAY'S manner is a mixture of habitual social
deference and a new-found assurance. "*At* your service,
sir."

68

THE COLONEL PLEADS

COLONEL WINSTANLEY: "I want a talk with you. I want a serious talk with you. As Chairman of the Bench and Deputy Lieutenant, *and* the former owner of a valuable collection of weapons, *and* the proprietor of a once powerful cellar, *and* the organiser of the Society for the Preservation of Law and Social Discipline here, and a fellow-citizen of our unfortunate constable, Winch, I naturally and properly want a talk with you. I want, if I may say so, an explanation—"

FOTHERINGAY: *"How*—I wish I knew. *Why*—it's almost as hard. All I know is I seem able to do things."

COLONEL WINSTANLEY: "And nice friendly things you do, eh?"

FOTHERINGAY: "Well you see—it's difficult to know what to do without offending people."

COLONEL WINSTANLEY: "Offending people! How the devil else could I take that trick about my whisky and my collection?"

FOTHERINGAY: "Well, Mr. Maydig—"

COLONEL WINSTANLEY: "Maydig—that new preacher chap! How does *he* come in?"

FOTHERINGAY: "Well, he was advising me."

COLONEL WINSTANLEY: "He was advising you!"

FOTHERINGAY: "And he thought for once if you went to bed sober—"

COLONEL WINSTANLEY: "Would you please say that again?"

FOTHERINGAY: "Well, if you didn't have too much to drink—"

COLONEL WINSTANLEY: "Go on, sir. Go on. I can bear it. I want to hear you out."

FOTHERINGAY: "And if we kind of made a symbolical change of all those swords of yours, it would sort of prepare your mind for the Peace of the World."

COLONEL WINSTANLEY: "And when may that be due?"

FOTHERINGAY: "Oh, almost at once—Peace—Plenty. Mr. Maydig made it very clear how we were to set about it."

COLONEL WINSTANLEY: "And you're going to set about it—when?"

FOTHERINGAY: "I'm going to see him about twelve and I suppose we shall start the Golden Age somewhen in the afternoon."

The COLONEL has become ominously calm. He speaks to the garden. "They are going to start the Golden Age somewhen—this afternoon." He addresses himself to the sky and universe, and speaks with great deliberation: "They . . . are . . . going . . . to . . . start . . . the . . . Golden . . . Age . . . somewhen . . . this . . . afternoon."

He turns to Fotheringay. "Under the circumstances I hardly like to mention my collection and my whisky."

FOTHERINGAY: "Don't mention it. We reely didn't mean to annoy. I'll put it right now." Gesture and inaudible words.

COLONEL WINSTANLEY: "Is that all you do? Just that?"

FOTHERINGAY: "That's all."

COLONEL WINSTANLEY: "And the miracle done. And my whisky is whisky. And the collection back."

FOTHERINGAY: "We can go and see it. The extraordinary thing is I *can* do these things. I could turn this garden into a palm tree forest and fill it with tigers. There reely doesn't seem to be a limit to what I can do."

70

The COLONEL surveying him: "There isn't a limit to what you can do! *You!*"

FOTHERINGAY: "Me. It just comes out of me."

COLONEL WINSTANLEY: "You can do practically anything?"

FOTHERINGAY: "Well, would you like me to do anything?"

The COLONEL aghast: "But a fellow of your sort!"

FOTHERINGAY, betraying a latent irritation: "Well, why shouldn't it be a fellow of my sort? Do you *want* to see a miracle? Something big?"

COLONEL WINSTANLEY: "Perhaps it's just as well to know what one is up against."

FOTHERINGAY: "Like to see India again? Like a glimpse of—what's some Indian place? Bombay. Let us both be in Bombay."

Scene changes to a crowded place in Bombay.

FOTHERINGAY: "Well, Colonel?"

COLONEL WINSTANLEY rubs his eyes: "You can do a thing like this?"

FOTHERINGAY: "Nobody else did it. Are you satisfied you are in Bombay?"

COLONEL WINSTANLEY: "The place has changed a lot. But I recognise it. Yes, I admit it; we're in Bombay. And how the devil we shall get back, Heaven knows. I had to talk to some men after lunch."

FOTHERINGAY: "Very well. You shall talk to them. We won't stay here. Let us be back in the Colonel's garden at Dewhinton. Now."

They return to the garden scene.

MAN WHO COULD WORK MIRACLES

FOTHERINGAY: "Well, sir? Is it all right, can I work miracles or can't I?"

COLONEL WINSTANLEY: "No doubt of it. Talk about abolishing distance!"

They move towards the house in silence.

Dissolve as they go up the garden.

The scene changes to the hall of the Colonel's house. Everything is in order. The Colonel and Fotheringay are continuing a conversation that has evidently been going on for some time. The Colonel is sitting on a hall table. Fotheringay stands still or walks a little to and fro.

FOTHERINGAY: "Mr. Maydig, you see, he has Ideas. He has Imagination. Now there isn't much sense—seeing these Gifts that have come to me—in going on with business and banking and all that. Mr. Maydig calls that a Want System—and now we are going to live in a Plenty System. There's no need for people to be hard up now. No need for people to be sick and ill and hungry. No need for robbing and cheating. And no need for war."

COLONEL WINSTANLEY: "No need for *anything* so far as I can see."

FOTHERINGAY: "Well, it will be *different*. But Mr. Maydig says you can't work miracles and stay as you are."

COLONEL WINSTANLEY: "And if you put an end to war, sir,—as I gather you intend to do before tea-time to-day —and I am beginning to believe you can—if you put an end to competition, make work unnecessary, give everybody more money than they can spend, then I ask you:

What are people going to DO, sir? What are they going to *do?*"

FOTHERINGAY, simply and candidly: "You know that's where *I'm* puzzled. But Mr. Maydig, he thinks we ought to just go about Loving one another."

This is too much for COLONEL WINSTANLEY. He jumps down from the table and roars: "Go about *loving* one another! Go about *loving* one another! Are you mad, sir? Are you human? Have you no sense of decency? The most private—the most sacred feelings!"

FOTHERINGAY: "Mr. Maydig seemed to see it so differently. Of course, there's art and science and making things."

COLONEL WINSTANLEY: "Fretwork and—" He gasps apoplectically. "Fretwork and foolery!"

FOTHERINGAY: "I suppose we can give it a trial. We don't properly know what human beings *will* do, Mr. Maydig says."

COLONEL WINSTANLEY gives way to rage. "Mr. Maydig says! Mr. Maydig says! And you're launching this bedlam millennium of yours in about six hours from now. What is going to happen to us all? What will become of us?"

FOTHERINGAY: "I reely don't know exactly myself. It'll be a bit of a change. Mr. Maydig says—"

COLONEL's frantic gesture: "Oh!" He walks some steps from Fotheringay, glances at a particularly sinister Malay kreese on the wall, hesitates for a moment and then by a great effort of self-control comes back to parley with Fotheringay.

COLONEL WINSTANLEY: "Now, look here, Mr. Fotheringay, won't you give all this business a few hours'—a few days' consideration, before you—before you let rip. Here we are. We've built up a sort of civilisation. People fit into it."

FOTHERINGAY: "Not so perfectly."

COLONEL WINSTANLEY: "At any rate they get along. We've got the Empire. A kind of order."

FOTHERINGAY: "That's all very well for people like you. But most people in the world are people like me. It's natural for you to want to keep things as they are. But I'm all for letting them loose. See? I don't *mind* change. I think change may be a Lark."

COLONEL WINSTANLEY: "Hasn't there been enough change in the last hundred years, railways, electricity, photography, steel ships, radio?"

FOTHERINGAY: "It's shook us up a bit but it hasn't killed us. I'm all for More and Better Change."

PART XIII

Man of Action

THE scene is the Colonel's study. It is afternoon. The Colonel has changed his garden clothes and is smoking a cigar. With him are Grigsby, Bampfylde, the Superintendent of Police, a vicar, a young gentleman in a very horsy get-up. They have been given coffee, cigars, liqueurs and after lunch refreshment.

The Colonel in a state of plethoric excitement, dominates the scene. But the others are in substantial agreement with him.

COLONEL WINSTANLEY: "You don't seem to see how serious it all is! While we are sitting here in our old homes and our old habits and following our old ways, these two dangerous lunatics are going to change the world—change us and everything. Can anything stay as it was? I ask you. You know their business ideas, Grigsby?"

GRIGSBY: "He'll kill business."

BAMPFYLDE: "He'll kill credit. The human world is held together by a cash nexus and if that goes—everything goes."

COLONEL WINSTANLEY: "And he'll leave the country open and unarmed to anyone who chooses to start an air raid. This measly-looking little draper chap is the most dangerous lunatic that ever got loose. I tell you, Mr. Smithells,—law or no law—you'll have to arrest him."

SUPERINTENDENT: "Well—if I try it—? Motor criminals are bad enough for the local constabulary, but if we are to deal with *miracle* criminals. It's beyond us—Colonel, and I warn you."

The COLONEL now becomes most important and the camera comes towards a close-up. "It's beyond us."

"Well, I'm all for law and order—under normal conditions.

"But are these normal conditions? Sometimes there is such a thing as drastic action or none. Sometimes still —a man must take a risk and break the law. Gentlemen, I don't ask you to share my responsibilities. Only maybe *later*—"

The Colonel's face takes on a look of stern resolution.

"These men are mad dogs. They have to be treated like mad dogs. It is our world and all that is worth while—against their confounded antics.

"If one happens to see red—if one happens to see red.

"There's such a thing as justification."

He turns away and the camera comes round to see him walk out of the room, and follows him as he strides down the hall, receding down a vista. No one moves until Bampfylde stirs and nods slowly and understandingly to Grigsby. Then both look at the superintendent, who remains enigmatic at attention. The vicar affects to be lost in thought. The young sportsman cranes his neck to follow the Colonel's movements.

The back of the Colonel is seen looking at a sporting gun on the wall. Then very deliberately he takes it down and examines it. But it will not do. No. He wants a bullet, not buckshot. He gets down a service rifle. He goes to a cabinet and takes out cartridges. Sharp clicks as he loads the gun. All this is done with his back to the audience. Fade out.

PART XIV

Doubts on the Eve of the Millennium

SCENERY. Some very pleasant sunlit meadows near Dewhinton. A river. Willow trees, running water and Dewhinton church amidst a clump of elms in the distance.

Enter Maydig and Fotheringay walking in a leisurely fashion. Maydig leads and talks. Fotheringay conveys an effect of being drawn along after him.

MAYDIG: "What a perfect afternoon! And to think it is New Year's Eve for the world. We are on the verge of the greatest change this Earth of Ours has ever seen. Want will vanish and Plenty reign. Ring out the Old, Ring in the New. . . . You know it is just as though I wanted to loiter a little—before the Beginning and the End."

They sit down on a fallen log.

MAYDIG: "Silly old world, what a lesson you have to learn!"

FOTHERINGAY: "I wish I knew a bit more exactly what we are going to do. Last night I was thinking a lot. I'm not *clear* on all sorts of things yet."

MAYDIG: "Nor I. It is all one great shining cloud of hope."

FOTHERINGAY: "Yes. But I have to do my miracles in a sort of order—one after the other."

78

MAYDIG: "I realise that."

FOTHERINGAY: "There's this making everybody in the world perfectly healthy. I suppose that's all right?"

MAYDIG: "Gloriously, exuberantly healthy, why not?"

FOTHERINGAY: "Well. They'll bounce about a bit. I suppose you *can* have human bodies perfectly healthy—and they'll still work?"

MAYDIG: "Certainly. Why not? Drawn by pleasure instead of driven by pain."

FOTHERINGAY: "What is perfectly healthy?"

MAYDIG: "We shall see."

FOTHERINGAY: "The doctors won't like it. It's *their* business to make us healthy. They won't like us to cut in on them."

MAYDIG: "Don't tell me, Mr. Fotheringay, don't tell me! Don't tell me that doctors do not want the whole world to be one glowing mass of health."

FOTHERINGAY: "Do I *need* to tell you? Those doctors —they'll have nothing left but their appetites."

Maydig features moral horror.

FOTHERINGAY: "But it's all like that. People are used to living in a certain way. That's what Mr. Grigsby and Mr. Bampfylde mean. If we give everybody plenty of money and plenty of everything—won't it be a bit like winning without playing a game? What are people going to DO?"

MAYDIG: "There will be plenty to do—plenty."

FOTHERINGAY: "What?"

MAYDIG: "Oh! we can arrange property and production and trade and money so that there will still be plenty of things to do."

FOTHERINGAY: "Yes, but we haven't settled how we are going to do that."

MAYDIG: "Matters of detail. And then as to this question of leisure. It's been raised already by science and invention and rationalisation and all that. It's not a *new* question. You and your miracles are only hurrying things on a bit. Scientific progress has warned us already. The answer is the intelligent pursuit of happiness, artistic work, creative energy."

FOTHERINGAY: "But that's where the Colonel comes in. Mr. Maydig, d'you think people—people as a general rule—want to go in for artistic work and all that?"

MAYDIG: "We must *make* them want."

FOTHERINGAY: "That's just where *my* miracles stop. I can't get *inside* people; I've tried it a bit. I can turn them upside down, send them to San Francisco in a jiffy, heal their diseases, make them rich—but people remain people."

MAYDIG: "An individual remains an individual."

FOTHERINGAY: "I suppose that's how you'd put it."

MAYDIG: "But you can affect them indirectly. Healthier people are happier people. Easier people are kindlier people. People who are not vexed or driven are better."

FOTHERINGAY: "Yes. To a certain extent. To a certain extent. But then won't a lot of new—desires get loose? Mr. Maydig, I've got some powerful desires. As I feel this power in me, they seem to grow."

MAYDIG: "Ah, my young friend! How often it has been my lot to hear that confession from young men in their strength. I know. I understand. We all have those powerful desires. Even in my own case—"

His expression is of one who experiences a rush of memories.

FOTHERINGAY: "Never mind about *your* case. It's *my* case I'm talking about."

MAYDIG: "I can assure you there is nothing singular about you."

FOTHERINGAY: "Exactly. That's where the trouble will come in. If everybody's like me—"

MAYDIG: "The guidance, the mastery of desire is a pure love."

FOTHERINGAY: "I *got* a pure love."

MAYDIG: "Then?"

FOTHERINGAY: "It isn't enough. There's that girl Maggie Hooper, who told me to come along and see you."

MAYDIG: "I know her. A very pure, simple, sensible girl."

FOTHERINGAY: "That's her. I'm very fond of her. That's all right. But the girl—the sort of girl that sets me *wanting*, isn't her."

He stands up.

MAYDIG: "Dear, dear! Wandering of desire. You must restrain it."

FOTHERINGAY: "Well, why *should* I? I happen to want a girl called Ada Price. Maggie sews on my buttons and mends my socks. She's perfectly lovely when she is sewing on buttons and mending socks. But there's a sort of 'Come and Take me' about Ada Price—"

MAYDIG also standing and assuming a pulpit manner: "The trouble is as old as the hills. Resist temptation. Let your motto be Service."

FOTHERINGAY: "Why should it be? *Why* Service? Why should *I* go about making people healthy and beautiful and get nothing out of it? Why should I let Bill Stoker, blast him, get away with it?"

MAYDIG: "My *dear* Friend!"

FOTHERINGAY: "And that's what most people are going to say! All this Power—it's going to let me loose. All these miracles of Speed and Plenty and Health, they're going to let most people loose. 'Come and Take me'—*that* stirs us."

PART XV

Death Comes into the Picture

SAME grouping.

A rifle shot is heard. The tearing whine of a bullet follows. Fotheringay's hat flies off and he puts his hand to his head, which is hurt. He stares in astonishment at his blood-stained fingers. The whine of a second bullet follows and a twig of an overhanging tree is shot off.

"They're shooting at us," cries MAYDIG. "Lie down," and he goes promptly flat on his stomach. But Fotheringay remains standing.

FOTHERINGAY: "Stop that! Stop any more bullets."

The blood comes pouring down his cheek.

FOTHERINGAY: "No bullets to hit me. Nothing to hurt me. And the wound on my scalp, stop bleeding and be well again."

But his face and his hand are still smeared with blood and remain so throughout this scene, giving his face a certain forcible strangeness.

FOTHERINGAY: "Me, be invulnerable. See? *Now!* Ah!"

He has thought and realised and changed with great rapidity. From now on, there is real force in his bearing. His last traces of deference and hesitation have gone.

FOTHERINGAY: "And now, let's see who fired that shot.

I want a word with him. 'Ere, you over there! Let your gun barrel be solid now!"

He stops. He looks at Maydig who rises slowly on all fours, looking back at him. The two confront each other but they are no longer even pretending to be master and pupil.

FOTHERINGAY: "Stand up, Maydig. . . . And that's all this silly world can do to a man who can work miracles! Who meant nothing better than to do things for it. Healing their illnesses! Giving them plenty! Making them free! Tried to cheat me out of my life! Tried to stop me. I suppose—" He figures with his finger out before him. "—I suppose another inch would have settled me. . . . Now let's go and see who did the shooting. I think I can make a pretty good guess."

MAYDIG: "And I."

They start off together. Maydig has the longer legs but something obliges him now to let Fotheringay lead the way.

MAYDIG: "I suppose—wouldn't it be well to make me invulnerable too?"

FOTHERINGAY looks at him for a moment: "All in good time, Maydig. But just for a bit, I'll look after you. So long as I am safe—trust me—everything is safe."

Change to the colonel behind a thick and flowery hedge. Honeysuckle and wild roses. He watches through the branches the two advancing. He shakes his fist at them. Across a broad field Maydig and Fotheringay are seen approaching. The colonel raises his rifle as if to shoot and finds it useless.

COLONEL: "This is too much." He mutters. "Take

cover." He throws down his rifle and crouches down.

Return to the grim face of Fotheringay advancing. Then to Maydig behind him. Maydig apprehensive and subdued. They advance, striding nearer and nearer. The top of the hedge comes into the picture. Maydig and Fotheringay look down over the hedge into the field.

FOTHERINGAY: "Where is he?"

Maydig and Fotheringay scramble over and through the hedge and look about them. The colonel has disappeared. His abandoned gun lies on the thick grass.

MAYDIG: "He's fled! At any moment he may shoot again."

FOTHERINGAY: "He can't."

MAYDIG: "I hope most sincerely he can't. If *I* were invulnerable . . ."

FOTHERINGAY: "But where *is* he?" He looks at the hedge and has a new inspiration. " 'Ere! All of you—you roses and honeysuckle and nettles and grass—all of you. Answer. Speak up! Where is he?"

Close-up of the WILD ROSES. They speak in hoarse, thin voices: "He's in the ditch to the left."

Close-up of the NETTLES. They speak in acid tones: "He's in the ditch to the left."

Close-up of the HONEYSUCKLE. Its voice is sweet: "He's in the ditch below me."

Close-up of the GRASS below. A flat herbaceous voice rather like Greta Garbo's: "He's *here*."

The grasses part and the Colonel crawls slowly out of the ditch; remains on all fours for a moment resentfully and then gets up.

MAN WHO COULD WORK MIRACLES

COLONEL, with a grimace: *"Kamerad!"*

FOTHERINGAY: "I thought it was you. None of the others would have been as outright as that. You are a man of action. I *knew* it was you."

COLONEL: "There's no fighting against miracles. Well, well. You've got to work your silly monkey tricks, I suppose. I tell you I'm sorry I didn't get in with that first shot. And now, get on with Mr. Maydig's magic millennium and see how you like it."

FOTHERINGAY: "No."

COLONEL: "You don't mean to say you've had a gleam of sanity!"

FOTHERINGAY: "I've been learning fast and hard, colonel, for two days. Perhaps there won't be a millennium. Perhaps there can't be. 'Ere's Maydig, he's got no end of ideas . . . but I've got my feelings . . . and it's me that has to put them through."

MAYDIG: "But you don't mean to give up all the things we've talked about. Just because he tried to shoot you."

FOTHERINGAY: "Not that."

MAYDIG: "And because your own desires are strong!"

FOTHERINGAY: "It isn't only that. Some of your things I shall do and some I shan't. *I* can work miracles—*I!* It's *me* has the Power. This isn't the world of Colonel Winstanley any more. It isn't the world of Grigsby or Bampfylde or anyone else. And it isn't going to be the world of the Reverend Silas Maydig neither. It's going to be the world of George McWhirter Fotheringay D.G., and as I want it so it will be, and what I want I get. All of you—you wanted just to use me. Now I'm going to use myself."

DEATH COMES INTO THE PICTURE

MAYDIG: "What for?"

FOTHERINGAY: "For getting exactly what I fancy. That's the natural human thing to want and that's what I want. See?"

Fotheringay's face has darkened and become much more forcible.

"I'm about beginning to get the hang of this miracle business. You've all had your say. The only chap who's got near to common horse-sense about it is Bill Stoker— and that won't do *him* much good by the time I've done with him. Come along, Maydig. I may want you. We're going to start the world of George McWhirter Fotheringay right 'ere in the Colonel's house."

Group receding towards the village. Fotheringay leads, dictatorially musing. Maydig walks at his elbow. He is engaged in silent colloquy with himself and occasionally shakes his head. The Colonel follows sullenly with his useless gun some paces behind.

Ominous music.

Half-length of Fotheringay *en face* brooding, thinking in the rhythm of the music. With the others following.

PART XVI

The Soliloquy

THE Colonel's bed-room. Manly accessories. Riding-boots and spurs. Regimental officers' photographs. Pistols on night-table. A cheval-glass. The door opens and FOTHERINGAY appears. He speaks to someone unseen (Maydig) outside door. "I want to be alone for a bit 'ere. Shan't be long."

He shuts the door on the outer world.

FOTHERINGAY: "You've got Power, George McWhirter, and you can't run away from Power. Got Power? . . . Power's got *you*."

He comes to a pause facing the cheval-glass. His hands are in his pockets. "Blood on my face?"

He feels it.

He begins to grimace in front of the glass, folds his arms like Napoleon; then makes an eloquent gesture, arm out.

FOTHERINGAY: "Let me be a little taller and bigger."

The change is effected. He is standing with his back to the audience and the mirror shows his face. It and the room become relatively about one-fifth smaller than before.

FOTHERINGAY: "If I had a higher forehead and a

harder mouth—. Let me have a high forehead and a harder mouth.

"Stronger eyes and dark eyebrows."

The mirror shows these changes.

FOTHERINGAY: "Straighter nose and a good moustache."

Long scrutiny of his reflection. "You look a queer chap now. But you aren't me. I don't like you somehow. No, let me be just as I was before I began changing. It's a queer thing, George McWhirter Fotheringay, seeing what a mug you are and what a mug you look, that you don't reely want to be anybody but George McWhirter Fotheringay. You just want to be yourself—until something wipes you out.

"I wonder did anyone *ever* want to be anyone but himself?"

He turns away from the mirror and interrogates himself earnestly. "What do I really want? I can have all the wishes in the world. What do I really want?

"Do I want Ada? I do. And *what* do I want of her? I want her to see I'm Master of the World, I want her to *feel* I'm master and show it—and when she's got that—do I want her any more? Not a bit of it. And Maggie? Maggie too. Instead of all this persuading me and helping me. I want to be Boss and lord of things, and so does everyone in his heart. But I, mind you, have Power. When I didn't realise I had it, I sang small. But not now. Oh! the Colonel be blowed, old stick-in-the-mud! and Grigsby, the tradesman, be blowed and Bampfylde be blowed. And Maydig be blowed! Maydig in *particular* be blowed. Tell me what to do, he would. Wise advice! Warnings! Ex-hortations. Who wants all this Progress and Service and doing things for other people, and going without oneself? Humbug! Humbug! They want *their* games and I want *my* game. I'll do things for them perhaps—but they'll have to be grateful to me. So we come down to hard tacks at last—it's Me—me, and *more* of me—and *most* of me—George McWhirter Fotheringay!"

Close-up of his excited and glowing face advancing with an effect of exultant menace towards the audience.

PART XVII

The World of George McWhirter Fotheringay

SCENE. The hall of the Colonel's house.

Maydig and the Colonel hover restlessly. Their mutual aversion is evident. They do not speak. The Colonel is still perplexed and worried by his gun barrel. He takes down some old pistols and examines them. Their barrels also have become solid. Maydig frets up and down, whispers and gesticulates to himself and watches the door through which Fotheringay must come. To them enter BAMPFYLDE who asks: "Has anything more happened?"

COLONEL: "My God! What *hasn't* happened? He's mad and dangerous, and bullets won't kill him."

The study door at the end of the hall opens and Fotheringay appears. His face is deadly white and lit up with excitement.

He approaches the three slowly with a certain air of menace. They do not move; they are in a state of great tension; they wait for him to speak first.

FOTHERINGAY: "I've got my own Ideas at last. This old world of yours—it's over. There's going to be a New Miraculous World. And it's going to be *Mine!*"

BAMPFYLDE: "You have the Power, sir—but—"

FOTHERINGAY: "Any objection?"

BAMPFYLDE: "Changes—even miraculous changes—can be too violent. There is such a thing as inertia."

FOTHERINGAY: "And what's this—*Inertia?*"

BAMPFYLDE: "It's a tendency in things to go on as they have been going. You can't even stop a motor-car *dead.*"

FOTHERINGAY with a slight grin: "Not without a miracle."

BAMPFYLDE: "You may think I am being needlessly obstructive, but people have to adapt themselves. You have to give them time. Hasten slowly. Advance circumspectly."

FOTHERINGAY: "And never get anything done! No. We begin 'ere and now. The world of George McWhirter Fotheringay. According to his dreams. According to what he's been told and found out since he began to think about things."

MAYDIG: "One word, sir. Whatever you may think of Mr. Bampfylde, you will at least admit that *I* am not unprogressive. I ask you—before you do anything else—Make a Plan. Nothing can be done without a Plan."

FOTHERINGAY screws his face up: "*What* Plan?"

MAYDIG: "Balance. Order. Creative aims."

FOTHERINGAY: "Plan! Talk away an age! Hesitate! Sway to and fro! Mess about! . . . I want my new world now. I want it to come in my life-time. While I can see it and glory in it and have some fun in it."

BAMPFYLDE: "Wait. Let things go on—just for a little while longer."

GEORGE McWHIRTER FOTHERINGAY

FOTHERINGAY smiles contemptuously at him: " 'Ere, let this house be changed to a great splendid beautiful palace and us in the great Hall of it. *Now.*"

Masterful sweep of the arm.

The four men remain grouped and the wainscotted narrow hall about them dissolves into a gigantic and beautiful interior. To the right are great windows lit up by the rays of the sun, sinking in the west. All that follows is to be grandiose and free from any trace of burlesque. The building can be something after the style of the Stockholm Town Hall. Or better, it can recall Paul Veronese.

FOTHERINGAY: "Not bad, eh? Architecture improving. But we hardly seem dressed for it. 'Ere, let us all be sumptuously dressed according to our characters and stations so as not to look strange here. Me, the Prince, Maydig and Bampfylde like Councillors, the Colonel as the Captain of the Guard. *Now!*"

The change is effected. The costumes can be futuristic—Renaissance—but they must not be extravagant or absurd.

FOTHERINGAY: "You'll like being Captain of the Guard after a bit, Colonel. Looks empty 'ere. What's your regiment, Colonel? Let his old battalion be 'ere and dressed accordingly. Now." (Guards appear.) "And let's have all the butlers and footmen in Essex 'ere as attendants—in suitable clothes. Same style as the building. Sort of rich like. So. Now 'ere's a place I can work in. Room to turn round in it. Not bad, is it? You didn't think I liked things Large. You saw to it that I was born small and grew up small. Nobody likes being

93

small. . . . Let's have a tame panther or two—five *tame* panthers, really tame, mind you—strolling about. I've always had a fancy for panthers. And a couple of elephants wouldn't look bad down there. Let there be two elephants there, all dressed up—driver and all complete." (Miracle gesture.)

FOTHERINGAY: "And now let us have 'ere Miss Ada Price, just as she was yesterday afternoon when I gave her a tiara and made her lovely."

Ada Price appears as Venus-Cleopatra.

FOTHERINGAY: "Well, Ada, my dear, and what do you think of it?"

ADA, surveying the scene: "Why!—there's Colonel Winstanley! All dressed up rich and handsome! This is something *like* a miracle. You're going it, George, at last. Where's *Bill?*"

FOTHERINGAY is stung: "Can't you do without Bill for a moment?"

ADA: "I thought you'd have Bill about—somehow. All this is sort of his style."

FOTHERINGAY controls himself by an effort: "It's *my* style, Ada."

He thinks: "Nothing to sit on? Let there be two thrones here."

They appear.

ADA: "You might have a throne for Bill."

FOTHERINGAY: "No. And that throne isn't for you. Just you stand down there, Ada—that's your place. . . . Let Maggie Hooper be dressed like a queen and let her come 'ere."

Maggie appears. Maydig, who has been watching

events with apprehension, becomes more confident and takes a step nearer.

FOTHERINGAY: "Well, Maggie, 'ere we are beginning the Miraculous Reign of George McWhirter Fotheringay. What shall we do with the world?"

Maggie is too overcome by amazement to speak.

ADA: "Oh! don't make it dull and goody-goody. . . . George, I didn't mean to say that about Bill! I didn't."

FOTHERINGAY, grimly: "But you said it. No. There's plenty of your sort. You just stand about being lovely—until I take notice of you. And just to keep you company, let the six next prettiest girls in Dewhinton come here—all lovely and beautifully dressed too. Not too much dressed. . . . My world's going to be full of pretty women, ten a penny."

A group of ladies appears. They appear with an expression of astonishment, look about them and whisper to one another overawed. They become aware of each other's beauty and an overpowering desire to see themselves in mirrors possesses them. One only carries a hand-mirror and this is much in request.

MAGGIE: "Dear George, make the world happy. Don't make it selfish and showy. Let this be really the world's great age."

MAYDIG, still growing in confidence: "Begins anew. Justice. Peace. Plenty."

FOTHERINGAY to Bampfylde: "You think I don't know how to do it. Now you shall see. Nothing in a hurry and nothing delayed. I've learnt a lot these three days—I begin to get the hang of it all."

MAYDIG: "Oh, take thought. Take counsel."

Fotheringay turns to him with a gesture between reassurance and mockery. He intends to take counsel—in his own fashion.

The camera comes round so that Fotheringay stands in half-profile at the head of a great system of staircases with the vast empty space of the palace court before him. Maggie, Ada, Maydig, Bampfylde, the Colonel are grouped about him. Other Councillors appear close to him as the scene proceeds. The camera comes up to his dark profile, beyond which the wide brightly-lit hall is shown.

FOTHERINGAY: " 'Ere. Let this Hall stretch so as to be big enough to hold all the people I am going to have 'ere. Let two hundred of the greatest bankers come 'ere and stand 'ere." (A number of rather amazed gentlemen appear.) "There you are. Let the thousand leading men who direct and own great businesses, stand 'ere." (The floor begins to be crowded.) "Let the chief men who rule people, the kings and presidents and politicians and commissars, the men who tell the newspapers what to say, the people who teach and preach. Let them come—yes—five thousand of them. *Now*."

The Hall far below is rapidly filled with a great multitude of men (and a few women) mostly middle-aged and respectable-looking people. A few priests in robes, a few uniforms are among them. Indian leaders. Chinese generals. Japanese, old style and new. It is *Who's Who;* it is *Who's Who in America;* it is *Europa* and the *Statesman's Year Book* assembled. They have the habitual self-control of men and women accustomed to be seen in public and watched by crowds. They stroll about in a slightly dazed way, accost one another, ask questions and gradually become aware of Fotheringay. The camera can wander over their upturned faces and show a selection of the intellectual life of humanity, in very slight caricature, all looking up at last to Mr. George McWhirter Fotheringay.

FOTHERINGAY: "Now 'ere we are for a great big talk together. I'm just anybody and you are the people who run the world. I've been told to take thought—take council. So I've got you to come 'ere! All of you! Why not?"

He pauses a little out of breath. Goes on with a certain strain in his voice. "Now I've got you. Now I've got the lot of you. All you what have your faces in the papers and sit in high places and walk through crowds of people and get all the cheers and praise! I've got you people who run the world *'ere,* to tell you to run it better. See—" His voice rises in excitement—"RUN IT BETTER."

Close-up of faces of representative prominent men at this announcement.

FOTHERINGAY pauses and then begins to scold: "You're the people who've lived on the fat of the world. You've been *trusted* with the world. Chaps like me have had to trust you, willy-nilly. And what sort of deal did you give us? What did you do for us, for all the trust we gave you? Science made miracles, if I didn't. There was plenty and more than plenty. The papers said so. The professors said so. *You* could go anywhere and do anything. And what did you do for *us?* What was *our* share?"

Protesting faces and cries from statesmen and journalists. An inaudible economist makes explanatory gestures.

"Oh, I know. I had to wait. Wait. Wait. Wait young and seedy—until I got old and seedy. And did. Be patient for umpty years while you held all the stuff in your hands—and did nothing. Much your crowd cared. Did you worry about it? Not a bit. But *you'd better worry now.*"

Close-up of indignant group. Uniformed soldier with his hand on revolver.

FOTHERINGAY's finger points to him: "No good shooting at me. I've *been* shot at. It won't work any more. There's an end to shooting. You can't shoot the truth. I'm 'ere and I've come to stay. George McWhirter Fotheringay! Power's gone out of your hands. You can strut about for a bit more and try to look important and play the old tricks, but I tell you Power has gone out of your hands." (Points to the sunset outside the great windows.) "That is *your* sun setting. It's late afternoon for the whole crowd of you. You know it. Gaw!—You try to make an excuse for it. Where has it gone, this Power? It's come to *me,* a common vulgar fellow, and it's driven me wild; it's come to me by a miracle."

Shots of the crowd in unison very intent. Then back to Fotheringay's profile and his gesticulating hand.

"And now you've got to do something, and do it soon. Make a new world that will make me happy. Get together, you Important People down there, and try to *be* reely important for once. Talk it over with each other and talk real stuff. Do it quickly and do it now. What was that trouble you got into about property? Why is property a curse to nearly everybody instead of what you pretend it is, something to ginger us up for our common good? I had none. I don't understand property. But you *know* about it. Did most of you grab too much of it and use it wrong? Did you ever try to clear that up and put it right? And what went wrong with our money? *You* fiddled about with it. Well, if you didn't, you let a lot of rascals fiddle about with it. You stood in. You played little games against each other. Great fun for you. Money! What Mr. Bampfylde calls the life-blood of society—and did you keep it clean? Did you use all the leisure and advantages you had to make it work better? Not you. And why could you never stop war? You could have stopped war. Why, a hundred resolute men in high places who weren't afraid of a bit of brain work, could have stopped war for ever—any time in the last twenty years. But I guess you liked the bands and the spurs and the feathers too much. And you didn't think about chaps like me. Nice and pompous you looked, inspecting the troops—being saluted. And did you really forget about chaps like me? Not even that. Not even that much excuse. A few trenches full of dead chaps like me? *That* made you feel more real and important, eh?"

Pause with his lips shut, nodding his point home.

Camera picks out an assortment of generals and military men, a foreign minister or so, munition dealers wearing orders, etc. They interrogate one another mutely. Camera returns to Fotheringay.

FOTHERINGAY: "Well now—just clear it all up—*now*. See? While I wait. 'Ere and now. You shan't eat or drink,

99

you shan't leave this place until you've cleared up the muddle you've lived in and kept me in ever since I was born. That's what I've got to say to you. And if you don't do what I tell you, I'll wipe you all out—as a child wipes a slate. That's me. That's what I've found inside me since I began looking. That's what I've dug out of George McWhirter Fotheringay."

MAYDIG to Bampfylde: "He's gone completely mad!"

BAMPFYLDE to Fotheringay: "But they *must* have time to think about it."

FOTHERINGAY: "If I give them time, they'll waste it. They've had—*generations* of time. Their sort. What have they done? What were they doing when I called them 'ere?"

BAMPFYLDE: "But these things cannot be done instantly."

FOTHERINGAY: "They are going to be done—'ere and now. A good and happy world. A sensible world. Then, when I've got that off my chest, we'll see." (He glances with a sort of affectionate desire at the ladies in waiting.) "We'll see about what can be made of living."

BAMPFYLDE, trying to reason with himself as well as Fotheringay: "There is an inertia in things that drives us on."

FOTHERINGAY: "Inertia!—I'm always up against this inertia. There is a power in *me* that wants a change. I'm sick of your old world and its Inertia!"

MAYDIG: "But at least wait until to-morrow. The sun is setting. Give them the night to think and discuss."

FOTHERINGAY: "No hurry about the sunset. I can stop that sunset. I want my new world now."

A NEW COUNCILLOR close at hand speaks.

"You can't stop the sun in the sky, sir!"

FOTHERINGAY: *"What!* I tell you I can."

The NEW COUNCILLOR: "No, sir. All the planets will fly off into outer space and outer darkness."

FOTHERINGAY: "One might think you were a banker, to hear you talk."

The NEW COUNCILLOR: "I'm a professor of physics."

FOTHERINGAY: "Well, *I'll* stop the sun setting. I won't *have* it set. Not till I want to go to bed—after we've cleared things up.

The NEW COUNCILLOR: "But then you'd have to stop the earth rotating!"

FOTHERINGAY: "And I WILL. No, don't argue with me, Maydig, don't argue with me, anyone. There's a time when argument stops."

He clenches his fists and stamps his foot. He becomes frantic with passion.

" 'Ere, Earth, stop rotating *now! Now!* Stop!"

The music, which has been increasingly uneasy, rises to an immense thud, which leaves everything throbbing. Everything flies off into streaks. The vibrations change into a torrent of sound which returns into the grandiose motifs of the opening Sequence.

PART XVIII

The Last Moment

THE starry universe. The three great Spirits of the opening Sequence appear against the stars.

The Player sits and looks down at the earth. The two others look over his shoulder.

The undertow of music becomes more manifest, it rises gradually to a powerful throbbing.

The PLAYER: "What has happened?"

The OBSERVER: "He's stopped the world going round!"

The INDIFFERENCE: "Not—suddenly?"

The OBSERVER: "Yes."

The INDIFFERENCE: "Then everything loose has been flung about by its own inertia—and that is the end of your nasty little pets upon their silly little planet. Preposterous! What did I tell you? It's all over. Come."

PLAYER: "No, no. It's not over. *He's* still alive—he's got a charmed life. He saw to that."

The OBSERVER, bending down closer: "Hit! No, Miss! He's missed again. *That* nearly had him. He's certainly got a charmed life."

Transition effects: a moment of 'abstract film.' It slows down and resolves itself into a rush of concrete ob-

102

jects. The music now throbs and beats and storms at the ears of the audience. A torrent, a Niagara rush of flying objects sweeps across the screen, trees, buildings, machinery, ships, water, railway-bridges, mountain-masses, the world flung headlong through the air. The atmosphere also is wildly disturbed. Screaming gale. Torn clouds streaming out and vast glares and forks of lightning. Wild torrents of whooping music also. Crashes and crescendos.

Fotheringay is seen flying head over heels, head over heels, in this tornado of objects. He goes in loping jerks. The elephant from his court nearly hits him. A large obelisk misses him by a yard. The voice of the OBSERVER is heard remotely: "Hit! No! Miss."

FOTHERINGAY's voice comes in jerks: "Let everything be. As it was—a minute before—I went into the Long Dragon."

Momentarily swift arrest of the things flying in the air. They must all swing round like ships coming about, and then stream down into a rush of black and grey lines which immediately swirl about and become the opening village scene of Sequence II. It is the street outside the Long Dragon. Fotheringay is seen outside the inn door.

He stands scratching his head. He looks up at the sky. Was it a dream?

"Hold hard for a bit. We haven't done yet. These miracles! If it happens that I *have* been working miracles, at the word Go, let me not be able to work any more miracles ever. No more miracles. And forget all about it. Forget about it. Wipe it out. You can't control it. *Go!*"

The pillar of vibrating ebon darkness which endowed him with his gift, appears above his head, quivers in black splendour and passes up into the sky.

PART XIX

The Mighty Powers Make Their Comments

RETURN again to the three great Spirits of the opening Sequence.

The INDIFFERENCE: "So he wouldn't have your gift. He threw it back to you."

The OBSERVER: "But he destroyed his world first. Your silly little planet has had a narrow squeak, Brother. Look at them. Not a soul among them realises that a minute ago every one of them was hurled headlong and smashed to pieces and brought back to life by a miracle."

The INDIFFERENCE: "They know nothing. He said 'Forget it.' And what has your experiment shown, Brother? What did you get out of that sample man? Egotism and elementary lust. A little vindictive indignation. That's all the creatures have—or will have for ever. What can you make of them?"

The PLAYER: "They were apes only yesterday. Give them time."

The INDIFFERENCE: "Once an ape—always an ape."

The PLAYER: "You say they are all just egotism and lust. No. There was something in every one of those creatures more than that. Like a little grain of gold glittering in sand, lost in the sand. A flash of indignation when they think things are false and wrong. That's God-like. Dirt is never indignant. That's why they interest me."

The OBSERVER: "Their indignation is always selfish. They are in a mess. They were made by the mess. They are made for the mess. They are part of the mess. They will never get out of their mess."

The PLAYER: "But if I give them power, not suddenly but bit by bit. If I stir 'thought and wisdom into the mess to keep pace with the growth of power. Broaden slowly. Age by age. Give the grains of gold time to get together."

The INDIFFERENCE: "And in the end it will be the same. A story of inertia, a story long drawn out instead of swift and sudden. But petty to the end."

The PLAYER: "No. It will be different."

The INDIFFERENCE, incredulous: "You say No? Still you say No!"

The PLAYER: "Come back here in an age or so and you shall see. . . ."

PART XX

Da Capo

THE scene returns to the bar-parlour of the Long Dragon at Dewhinton. At first it is, as it were, transparent. For some moments, that is, the constellations shine through the scene and fade slowly and vanish imperceptibly. The characters are the same and posed in the same attitudes as they were at the point in Sequence II when FOTHERINGAY says: "A miracle, *I* say, is something *contrariwise* to the usual course of nature, done by power of will—something that couldn't happen, not without being specially willed."

TODDY BEAMISH: "So *you* say."

FOTHERINGAY: "Well, you got to 'ave a definition." (Appeals to cyclist.) "What do *you* say, sir?"

Cyclist starts, clears his throat and expresses assent.

Fotheringay appeals to Landlord Cox.

COX: "I'm not *in* this."

TODDY BEAMISH: "Well, I agree. Contrariwise to the usual course of nature. 'Ave it so. And what about it?"

FOTHERINGAY, pursuing his argument: "For instance. 'Ere would be a miracle. The lamp 'ere, in the natural course of nature, couldn't burn like that upsy-down, could it, Mr. Beamish?"

TODDY BEAMISH: *"You* say it couldn't."

FOTHERINGAY: "And you? Wah!—you don't mean to say—No?"

TODDY BEAMISH: "No. Well. It couldn't."

FOTHERINGAY: "Very well. Then 'ere comes someone, as it might be me, along 'ere, and he stands as it might be 'ere, and he says to this lamp, as I might do, collecting all my will—and I'm doing it mind you—I'm playing fair: 'Turn upsy-down, I tell you, without breaking and go on burning steady.' " (Pause.) "Well, there, you see, nothing happens!"

COX: "Nothing *could* happen like that. It wouldn't be sense."

FOTHERINGAY: "Exactly. And miracles aren't sense."

MISS MAYBRIDGE, busy wiping out her beer-glasses: "All the same, I sometimes wish *I* could work miracles."

FOTHERINGAY, lounging: "I wonder what you'd *do* if you could work miracles."

MISS MAYBRIDGE: "Oh—I'd do lots of nice things." (Slight pause.)

TODDY BEAMISH: "I'd make the world a better place. Within reason."

They all follow their own train of thought for a second or so.

FOTHERINGAY becomes thoughtful; he makes the miracle gesture, but nothing ensues. "There's one or two things I'd like to do."

TODDY BEAMISH: "But you won't ever have the chance."

FOTHERINGAY, leaning half back to the bar and nodding his head a little ruefully. "No, I won't ever have the chance—Na-ow."

Close-up of his face—as though some phantom memory eluded him. "Na-ow." He lifts his hand and drops it again. Music swells, begins the miracle motif once more, loses heart and dies down to a sigh. Fade out slowly.

THE END